T0334576

Cambridge Elements ≡

Elements in the Gothic
edited by
Dale Townshend
Manchester Metropolitan University
Angela Wright
University of Sheffield

DEMOCRACY AND THE AMERICAN GOTHIC

Michael J. Blouin
Milligan University

CAMBRIDGE
UNIVERSITY PRESS

CAMBRIDGE
UNIVERSITY PRESS

Shaftesbury Road, Cambridge CB2 8EA, United Kingdom

One Liberty Plaza, 20th Floor, New York, NY 10006, USA

477 Williamstown Road, Port Melbourne, VIC 3207, Australia

314–321, 3rd Floor, Plot 3, Splendor Forum, Jasola District Centre, New Delhi – 110025, India

103 Penang Road, #05-06/07, Visioncrest Commercial, Singapore 238467

Cambridge University Press is part of Cambridge University Press & Assessment, a department of the University of Cambridge.

We share the University's mission to contribute to society through the pursuit of education, learning and research at the highest international levels of excellence.

www.cambridge.org
Information on this title: www.cambridge.org/9781009539111

DOI: 10.1017/9781009279932

First published 2024

A catalogue record for this publication is available from the British Library.

ISBN 978-1-009-53911-1 Hardback
ISBN 978-1-009-27997-0 Paperback
ISSN 2634-8721 (online)
ISSN 2634-8713 (print)

Democracy and the American Gothic

Elements in the Gothic

DOI: 10.1017/9781009279932
First published online: June 2024

Michael J. Blouin
Milligan University

Author for correspondence: Michael J. Blouin, MJBlouin@milligan.edu

Abstract: While the political undercurrent of the American Gothic has been firmly established, few scholars have surveyed the genre's ambivalent relationship to democracy. The American Gothic routinely undercuts centralised authority by exposing the dark underbelly of the status quo; at the same time, the American Gothic tends to reflect a widespread mistrust of the masses. American readers are too afraid of democracy – and not yet fearful enough. This concise Element theorises the democratic and anti-democratic elements of the American Gothic by surveying the conflicted imaginaries of the genre's mainstays, including Charles Brockden Brown, Edgar Allan Poe, Shirley Jackson, and Stephen King.

Keywords: Democracy, American politics, Gothic, horror, Stephen King

ISBNs: 9781009539111 (HB), 9781009279970 (PB), 9781009279932 (OC)
ISSNs: 2634-8721 (online), 2634-8713 (print)

Contents

1 Who's Afraid of Democracy?

Published in 1824, Washington Irving's 'The Adventure of the German Student' recounts the misadventures of a German student as he wanders around Paris in the aftermath of the French Revolution (**Figure 1**).[1] The distracted pupil comes across a beautiful woman at the foot of a bloodied guillotine, and they quickly profess their love for one another. It is, after all, a 'time for wild theory and wild actions'. The German student strikes an egalitarian chord when he boldly tells his *amour*, 'We are as one' (Irving 1998: 226). But when he wakes up the next morning, Irving's melancholy protagonist discovers – to his shock – that the object of his affection is, in fact, a decapitated corpse, reanimated 'to ensnare him' (227). Apparently, falling prey to a popular delirium that springs from democratic demands, the young man loses hold of reality, and so he must pay the price of a life in the madhouse. This unsettling message from one of early America's foremost writers speaks to anxious audiences two centuries later: when left unchecked, democracy leads to unspeakable horrors.

Yet if the shelves of popular booksellers are to be believed, contemporary American readers love democracy. They lament its perceived passing; they pine for its eventual realisation. Readers might assume, then, that the American Gothic and democracy have re-enforced one another across the generations, in that both modes, aesthetic as well as political, likely generate revulsion at the idea of oppressive monsters that threaten personal freedom. I could rehearse a lengthy list of repugnant tyrants from the (mostly British) canon: Horace Walpole's Manfred, Mary Shelley's Victor Frankenstein, Matthew Lewis's Ambrosio. Understandably, readers could be tempted to presume that the American Gothic is built upon a denunciation of destructive demagogues. The pages of American Gothic fiction ought to be populated by grotesque despots and express a sensationalised fear of democracies lost. But the story is not so simple because to oppose authoritarians does not automatically trigger an endorsement of democracy. Moreover, while many works in the American Gothic tradition are by default liberal, thanks to their reactionary protection of private property as well as their progressive focus on the survival of the hyper-individualist, the genre's critics have not fully unpacked the genre's unique connection to democracy. An exception to the rule, Alan Lloyd-Smith briefly ponders the 'anxieties about popular democracy' that manifest throughout the American Gothic (Lloyd-Smith 2004: 4). In the sections that follow, I want to explore these anxieties in greater detail. From Irving to Edgar Allan Poe, from H.P. Lovecraft to Stephen King, most of the dominant figures within the

---

[1] Henry S. Canby famously described Irving as 'the arch-Federalist of American literature' (Canby 1931: 86).

Figure 1 Washington Irving's German student encounters his lover in the shadows of the guillotine

American Gothic tradition act as naysayers of the nation's ongoing democratic experiments. Irving's beheaded spectre has long stalked the margins of American nightmares. In turn, the American Gothic ought to play a vital role in efforts to reclaim democracy, especially at the current moment in which America's democratic institutions stand at the threshold of a managerial re-entrenchment – or a radical re-imagining.

One reason for the blurriness of the line between adoration and dread of democracy may be lingering uncertainties regarding what the term 'democracy' actually means. In the twenty-first century, the concept of democracy has become ubiquitous. Democracy can be found everywhere (and so, oddly enough, nowhere). It ostensibly covers everything like a fine mist. Crafty politicos conjure its fetishised form, sleepwalkers fantasise about its regenerative powers, and countless prophets foretell its immanent destruction. But what lies beneath the surface of these paeans? Before its champions defend democracy, they must face up to how a significant percentage of Americans truly feel concerning their purported ideals. The time has come to inject a more thorough analysis of *fear* into ongoing debates about the future of democracy. After all, 'democracy puts its citizens under a strange form of psychological pressure by building them up as sovereigns and then regularly undermining each citizen's experience of sovereignty' (Allen 2004: 27). The fear of losing an election is a near constant. While many Americans sing songs of praise to the uplifting aspects of democracy, a careful listener hears mournful dirges dedicated to the anxiety of powers lost rather than gained. As this Element will show, the terrain of the American Gothic is a productive place to begin these conversations.

Based upon its initial Greek formulation, democracy means the power (*kratos*) of the people (*demos*). Since the early days in Athens, democracy has gradually come to mean the consent of the majority for certain representatives, a prioritisation of personal liberty, an investment in equality (one person, one vote), and an ongoing investment in interest groups mobilizing – that is, generating enthusiasm among – the masses.[2] For democracy to function, citizens-stakeholders voluntarily abide by a set of behavioural expectations colloquially described as 'democratic'. Eleanor Roosevelt described these values in a theological fashion: 'The Revolutionary idea, guided by religious feeling, [is] the basis of Democracy' (Roosevelt 2016: 33). Democracy is driven primarily by pathos. Still, the concept of a collective remains key: democracy signals a relentless pursuit of egalitarian ends since no single citizen counts more than any other, and the advantages of economic privilege must be countered by programmes that enhance political power for all. Jacques Rancière argues that democracy is 'the wrench of equality jammed (objectively and subjectively) into the gears of domination, it's what keeps politics from simply turning into law enforcement' (Rancière 2011: 79). In its brightest moments, democracy sews the seeds of greater dignity, self-worth, civic responsibility, mass franchise, tolerance for diversity, and a conciliatory sense of what all individuals hold in common. America's democratic project outwardly fuels itself on freedom as well as fraternity.

At the same time, democracy in practice means embracing dissatisfaction. No one will get everything they want, and because at its core democracy resists conclusive signification, a final arrangement that would require no further revisions, democrats must accept that any community remains comprised of individuals with variegated desires. There could never be a democracy that meets all of these criteria. A major proponent of democracy, Jean-Jacques Rousseau famously confesses: 'A genuine democracy never has existed' (Rousseau 2014: 213). Nor could it exist. Believers in democracy must therefore hold in tension the impossibility of their agenda with an enduring faith in its utopian promise. Michael Hardt writes, 'The democracy aimed for always exceeds the democracy practiced' (Hardt 2019: xxi). To which Astra Taylor adds, democracy offers 'a distant and retreating horizon, something we must continue to reach towards yet fail to grasp' (Taylor 2019: 13). It is this requisite

---

[2] For a succinct description of democracy, see Crick (2003).

uncertainty, this perpetual dependence upon the unknown, that alerts readers to the possibility of a meaningful relationship between democracy and the American Gothic.

Admittedly, Gothic voices harbour plenty of reasons to be sceptical of democratic idealism. Shortly after the birth of Athenian democracy, Plato chastised its practitioners for allowing 'the mob' to gain an upper hand over his vaulted Philosopher-King. Baruch Spinoza later concurred, observing that, since a population is mostly ill-educated, democracy quite literally means rule by the ignorant.[3] According to these canonical thinkers, members of the perceived rabble inevitably fall prey to charlatans who capitalise upon their passions. Let us pivot to democracy in an American setting: of note, the word democracy does not appear in the American Declaration of Independence, and the vast majority of early Americans were uneasy with the prospect of a democratic society. In young America, 'democracy was distrusted, even feared' (Bryan 2003: 25). To quote Toni Morrison: 'It is striking how dour, how troubled, how frightened and haunted our early and founding literature truly is' (Morrison 1992: 35). Following in the wake of the French Revolution, with its ghastly spectacles – Irving's feverish phantasm glides past once more – prominent Americans expressed trepidation at the idea that their nascent republic would soon enter into a revolutionary spiral, with its citizens succumbing to the drug of democratic zeal. 'Democracy became a virtual synonym for violent anarchy' (Miller 2018: 59). Even cultural celebrities later presumed to be vocal proponents of democracy often felt frightened by it. For example, Ralph Waldo Emerson once blamed democracy for creating a deficient society 'in which the members have suffered amputation from the trunk, and strut about so many walking monsters' (Emerson 2000: 44). For two centuries, democracy has been keeping Americans awake at night.

As I discuss in greater detail in the second section, Edgar Allan Poe frequently returns to the question of democracy. For instance, Poe's 'The System of Doctor Tarr and Professor Fether', a story set, like Irving's 'Adventure', in the revolutionary hotbed of France, follows an unwitting narrator as he visits an uncanny French asylum. The narrator eventually learns that the patients have overrun their captors and now run the institution. Poe's narrative offers a not-so-subtle critique of democracy. Initially, the reader encounters a sort of managerial democracy, a democracy that only superficially resembles its namesake; through what is called a 'system of soothing', the doctors 'secretly watch' the inmates yet leave them with 'much apparent liberty' (Poe 1984: 700). Unconvinced by this curated version of democracy, Poe's imprisoned mob

---

[3] For an in-depth analysis of Spinoza's attitude towards democracy, see Smith (2005).

grows increasingly cacophonous. By the end of the story, the asylum's innately unreasonable crowd has subscribed to the anarchical law of tarring and feathering its enemies, hence the pun of the tale's title. Pandemonium breaks out as Poe's rebel madmen imagine they have 'invented a better system of government', although, in truth, they have established a 'lunatic government' (713). Poe closed this Gothic burlesque by comparing the democratic mob, as he habitually did, to a band of primates. Following in Irving's footsteps, Poe's conventional Gothic plotline captures a widespread sense of dread regarding the fate of American democracy.

A good number of twentieth-century Americans were no less afraid of democracy than their predecessors. After Woodrow Wilson's time in office, presidential regimes minimised democratic feedback and slowly constructed a vast bureaucratic system that could counteract interference from a pesky electorate. Politicos wrote scathing treatises against what they called *rabies democratica*; in the early twenty-first century, Senate majority leader Mitch McConnell spread the campaign phrase 'jobs, not mobs' and worked tirelessly to secure a conservative Supreme Court, in an effort arguably designed to bypass the will of the people under the guise of serving that same general will. But conservative reactionaries are hardly the only ones afraid of democracy. In an age of climate change denialism and the election of fascist-leaning leaders, left-leaning voters regularly wax Platonic on the subject of democracy. Many leftists maintain that democracy is simply too slow to address the urgent threats that American society faces, while the stauncher Marxists in their ranks contend that 'a democratic republic is the best possible political shell for capitalism' (Lenin 2019: 10). Although, they contend, the act of voting has been treated like a panacea, as American consumers hear the near-constant harangue to vote more (an act that will magically solve everything), this proposed salve has not stemmed the tide of systemic horrors. On either end of the political spectrum, fears of democracy run rampant. America's trepidation regarding democracy returns regularly from its repression.

But this account may be a bit misleading. In some cases, I would argue that American audiences are not *excessively* afraid of democracy; in reality, Americans *may not yet be afraid enough*. Because democracy demands perpetual uncertainty – the open-endedness of ceaseless revolution; the endless disruption of a society empowered to redefine itself anew – a prominent Gothic element could help American democracy to function properly. That is, if citizens are not bone-chillingly fearful of what democracy means, they might be entirely too comfortable with a zombified version of democracy, one that is only half alive and therefore falls well short of its potential. To achieve their own revolutionary aims, perhaps Americans need to release the guardrails and plunge beyond the brink. In other words, to clear away failing institutions, democrats must come to terms with the true terror of the unknown. Accordingly, this Element explores a Gothic oscillation between reactionary horror and revolutionary terror: a generic paradox that conveys the consistently conflicted character of democracy in America.

Before turning to in-depth analyses of seminal texts in the sections to come, I would like to discuss briefly the illustrative example of the weird fiction of H.P. Lovecraft, a man who professed his appreciation for the anti-democratic tale by Irving that opened this introduction. Lovecraft was a well-known racist as well as an outspoken believer in social hierarchy. In one letter, he mocked 'apostles of equality' (Lovecraft 2005b: 27); in another letter, he stated: 'Democracy . . . is a false ideal – a mere catchword and illusion of inferior classes, visionaries, and dying civilizations' (qtd. in Joshi 1996: 321). Lovecraft's fiction doubles down on this mindset. His 1920 story 'The Street' erases the democratic rupture of the American Revolution by insisting that, in the wake of their revolutionary moment, Americans continued the conservative practice of 'speaking of the old familiar things in the old familiar accents' (Lovecraft 2019b: 71). Lovecraft's story overtly prioritises 'fine old traditions' above 'hideous revolution', and it casts multi-ethnic cooperatives, the very basis of a modern democracy, as inherently anarchical (73). Elsewhere, Lovecraft expressed his attraction to Gothic narratives with an anti-democratic message by critiquing Charles Brockden Brown's 'Godwinian didacticism' (William Godwin was a British radical democrat) while applauding Poe's 'anti-social qualities' (Lovecraft 2020: 26, 55). In short, Lovecraft's weird tales expose a simmering dread of democracy.

Lovecraft's short stories 'The Rats in the Walls' and 'The Horror at Red Hook' reflect their author's palpable fear of an egalitarian politics that empowers everyone, including people marked as belonging to different races and ethnicities. Many white readers and writers tend to fear direct democracy because direct democracy would cease forcing people of colour to shoulder so much political loss (voter suppression, economic disparity, gerrymandering, etc.). Lovecraft ostensibly cannot stomach the concept of a genuinely level playing field. In a broader sense, both of Lovecraft's weird tales emphasise the crumbling foundation of Western society, and this eroding foundation comes with specific sociopolitical associations. What is meant to be so terrifying to Lovecraft's reader about a Hellenic fundament? The answer lurks within one of the haunted vaults from 'Rats', in which the narrator recognises 'the severe and harmonious classicism of the age of the Caesars' (Lovecraft 2005c: 87). The entire haunted edifice was built upon the particular starting point of the age of the Caesars – an age that marked the transition from democratic-republican values to despotism. In effect, much like the fictional architectures of Irving and Poe, Lovecraft's unstable structures foretell the ruin of America's inherently populist premise. A good number of Lovecraft's stories depict democracy as an ill-fated substructure on which to build a world order.[4]

Lovecraft exposed a pestilential populace in order to demonstrate the grotesqueness of 'the people', an abject entity that Lovecraft held should never be trusted to govern itself. Simply put, Lovecraft cleaved the people (*demos*) from the power (*kratos*). Channelling Poe's 'The Pit and the Pendulum', a text discussed at length in the second section, Lovecraft's 'Rats' portrays a grotesque crowd that defies demands for greater social order. Significantly, 'Rats' highlights the unexpected death of American President Warren Harding as a 'horribly yawning brink', which is to say, as a site of tremendous uncertainty (Lovecraft 2005c: 95). Will democracy save the day or will the grotesque *demos* surge, like a pack of vermin, and tear the whole structure apart? Lovecraft's democracy seems destined to collapse as those timeless rats, a 'lean, filthy, ravenous army', storm the figurative Bastille: 'Their riot, stampeding [. . .] in numbers apparently inexhaustible' (82, 87). Lovecraft further stressed an unflattering depiction of the *demos* when he imagined a group of 'flabby', 'fungous' beasts, led by a possessed swineherd, in a correlation that foregrounds the Biblical story of Legion (88). 'Horror' offers yet another unsettling portrait of the people. In contrast to the 'pleasantness' of colonial times, Lovecraft's democratised Brooklyn unleashes 'a frightful and clandestine system of assemblies and orgies' (Lovecraft 2005a: 130). In Lovecraft's estimation, the free assembly of a diverse populace remains automatically terrible, secretive, and libidinal. Lovecraft's *demos* arrives in the form of a 'nightmare horde', a 'mad procession' led by 'baying dogs' (142–43). Lovecraft's life-long insistence on leaving his horrors unnamable could be read as a sign of the author's mistrust of the *hoi polloi*. Regarding the mysteries of 'Horror', Lovecraft's narrator insists that 'the world knew . . . all that it ought to know' (139). Repulsed by a pestilential people, Lovecraft sought refuge in his self-defined status as an isolated country gentleman.

Yet one could also read Lovecraft's anti-democratic horrors as a reactionary façade. Beneath the surface, these weird stories enable forward-looking audiences to tap into the terror of democracy's radical potential. The Lovecraftian sublime, the unspeakable beyond, triggers a palpable fear of what the aforementioned pests usher into being: an ontological rupture in the fabric of society; a shocking removal of the figurative floor beneath the status quo, manifested

---

[4] Even in his later years, during which he shifted into a perspective more aligned with socialism, Lovecraft never forfeited his preference for aristocracy. Lovecraft's 'distrust of democracy' extended into his calls, late in life, for intelligence tests as a barrier to voting (Joshi 1996: 572).

interchangeably as 'the assaults of chaos and the daemons of unplumbed space' (14). His prose recycles Gothic tropes to comprehend the pervasive fear of democracy in America, including, most prominently, chaotic pests and unplumbed pits, a composite that Lovecraft described as 'pest-gulfs' (Lovecraft 2019a: 287). 'Rats', for example, evokes 'a new pit of nameless fear' (Lovecraft 2005c: 95); meanwhile, 'Horror' gestures at a 'bottomless pit' that opens up to 'vistas of every realm of horror' (Lovecraft 2005a: 141). Lovecraft's use of the term vistas recalls Walt Whitman's democratic vistas, a concept that Whitman himself framed as nightmarish when, in the preface a book of the name same, he actively distanced himself from 'the People's rudeness, vice, caprices' (Whitman 2010: 4). At its most primal level, American democracy signifies the open-endedness of social arrangements. Below hordes of pestilent people, clamouring to have their demands met, Lovecraft unveiled the terror (or Terror with a capital T, to evoke the French precedent) of democratic revolution – or the abject terror of unplumbed pits. Excavating an important aspect of Lovecraft's texts, Patricia MacCormack underlines the emancipatory ruptures within Lovecraft's hierarchies, which she deems as openings for 'multiplicity and connectivity' – an alterity without any implied 'replacement structure' (MacCormack 2016: 199, 205). Lovecraft's pits undermine democracy by reminding his readers of democracy's eternally unfinished essence. In this sense, the inegalitarian author unwittingly cautioned his reader not to be excessively afraid of egalitarianism; instead, his weird fiction reveals Americans to be not yet fearful enough of democracy's potential. A Gothic theme, then: one relates to democracy like one relates to the omnipresence of death itself, being both irrationally horrified and maddeningly reserved at exactly the same time.

Much more than a superficial thematic concern, democracy materialises in the very structure of the American Gothic. Democracy is the political imperative that motors American narratives in the Gothic mode to their eventual resolution (or, more accurately, lack thereof). The book that follows remains indebted to Fredric Jameson's concept of the political unconscious as well as theoretical interventions by Rancière, Chantal Mouffe, and Ernesto Laclau. These theorists encourage readers to challenge the relatively facile paeans to democracy that have been sold to American consumers. Taking cues from these figures, I attempt to rethink the complicated relationship between democracy and fear through a sustained engagement with foundational Gothic texts.

As such, I situate myself in conversation with scholars that have turned to Gothic imagery to contemplate what ails American democracy. On one side, Richard Rorty, who declares a need for more Ralph Waldo Emerson and less Poe, claims that democracy has become entirely too Gothic, which for him means 'sadistic' and 'selfish' (Rorty 1997: 95). He argues that democracy has devolved into a paralyzed game of partisans that project monstrous opponents. On the other side, democracy *requires* fear, especially a fear of change. Indeed, a democracy without fear, if such a thing could ever really exist, would merely breed complacency and force its practitioners to go through the motions, under managerial types spouting platitudes. Bonnie Honig counters Rorty when she claims that American democracy is not yet Gothic enough, since its policy-making proponents prefer platitudes involving consensus and a facile resolution of differences to what Honig argues is a 'healthier' level of uncertainty, or citizens relating to one another 'gothically' (Honig 2001: 121). Is American democracy too Gothic, then, or not yet Gothic enough? To answer the question, this Element moves in two directions: it re-theorises American democracy through sustained engagement with the American Gothic and, at the same time, it re-theorises the American Gothic through engagement with American democracy. Democracy informs, and is informed by, the intimate shapes of the American Gothic, replete with claustrophobic crowds, ominous holes, torturous circles, and sublime vistas.

In sum, this Element holds that the anti-democratic streak of the American Gothic reflects a general unease in the populace with the promise of democracy, even as the Gothic mode offers a corrective by breaking unexpected pathways for a more democratic future. The trouble with certain defenders of democracy is that they tend to privilege the role of rationality in the upkeep of their preferred government model. When reciting a litany of pro-democracy talking points, democracy's most strident defenders prioritise 'reason, moderation, and consensus' (Mouffe 2000: 148). In actuality, American democracy more convincingly parallels the subversive nature of the Gothic, in that both democracy and the Gothic contest the cherished illusion of a well-ordered society by interjecting political possibilities back into a moribund social order. Placing democracy and the Gothic into conversation, this Element emphasises the central part that passion must continue to play in politics, while simultaneously teasing out democracy's innate dynamism – its conflicts, confrontations, and contradictions. In its most Gothic register, American democracy reveals that the ever-contestable character of politics cannot be repressed forever under 'the veil of rationality or morality' (Mouffe 2000: 150). Despite its reactionary origin, Irving's headless spectre could goad audiences into greater democratic engagement. In turn, proponents of democracy ought to reconsider the Gothic as an aesthetic tool with which to restructure stratified political imaginations and evade undue orderliness as well as barbarous hierarchies. The Gothic element of American democracy remains one of its most invaluable assets.

2 The Horrors and Terrors of a Radical Democracy

Democracy is more often curated than experienced in a living, breathing sense. Today, countless Americans consume staged town halls that have been scripted and manufactured in accordance with the results of algorithmic polling. Social media companies train users to treat their platforms as the equivalent of the Athenian public forum, when in fact these platforms were designed with the express intent of turning a profit.[5] As the historian Gordon Wood puts it, 'We Americans like to think of our revolution as not being radical', as 'essentially an intellectual event' and so 'hardly a revolution at all' (Wood 1991: 3–4). This problem is hardly new: since its inception in the era of Charles Brockden Brown and George Lippard (1790s–1840s), American democracy has been consistently choreographed and cleared of its political character. Precious few early Americans were permitted to vote and a plebiscitary approach to democracy prioritised well-endowed representatives, that is, elites with money and influence, to attain public office in lieu of direct forms of democracy. To many privileged individuals, the idea of an empowered electorate was nothing short of a nightmare.

In contrast to its meticulously managed twin, radical democracy upholds the terrifying kernel of the democratic promise – an ever-impending threat that 'the people' could unexpectedly rise to overturn the established way of doing things. Radical democracy holds open an empty place where centralised power would otherwise be, tracing the evasive outline of a better society to come in which power will be transferred from the select few to an ever more inclusive bloc. Although most citizens from this period did not possess the positive, if somewhat facile, connotations of democracy that would become ubiquitous in generations to follow, early Americans nonetheless worried about the fate of their democracy.[6] From Thomas Jefferson to Andrew Jackson, the spectre of a radical democracy haunted early America.

The spectre of a radical democracy perhaps manifested nowhere more visibly than in Philadelphia, the birthplace of the American Gothic as well as the sociopolitical backdrop against which Brown and Lippard set their respective Gothic texts. The constitutional convention of 1776 in Philadelphia, an event that produced results R.R. Palmer has since likened to the French constitution of 1793, became 'a symbol of what democrats meant by democracy', and it threatened to move the state of Pennsylvania much closer to something like

---

[5] Jacques Rancière articulates the central imperative: 'To evacuate politics, using the pincers of economic necessity and juridical rule' (Rancière 1999: 110).

[6] Ronald Formisano illustrates how by the 1790s a good number of Americans were already starting to fear 'too little democracy' (Formisano 2008: 27).

a direct democracy in which voters would engage in self-governance with fewer degrees of separation (Palmer 1969: 219). Sharing a state with the site of the Whiskey Rebellion of 1792, Philadelphia was home to the nation's largest free black population, the abolitionist Quakers, and countless 'communities of dissent that shaped the era's momentous struggle over the meaning of American democracy' (Jackson 2019: xiv). It was in Philadelphia in the year 1793 that America's first democratic societies emerged: groups dedicated to fighting for egalitarian social arrangements. Some Philadelphians experienced a reactionary horror at this possibility; other Philadelphians felt terrified by the prospect of such an unsettled state. For better or worse, the horrors and terrors of democracy were kindled by the Gothic works of Philadelphia's own Brown and Lippard.

Radical democracy found its initial expression in philosophical tracts by intellectuals with whom Brown and Lippard were well-acquainted, including the (in)famous Thomas Paine, another American figure forged in the revolutionary fires of Philadelphia. Paine's 1791 tract 'Rights of Man' tarries about the chasm of the unknown, evoking ontological rupture as the defining characteristic of any democratic order. 'Nothing of reform in the political world', Paine argued, 'ought to be held improbable' (Paine 1995: 540). Brown participated in many spirited debates about Paine's works. Initially celebrated for his revolutionary tracts, Paine's opponents eventually turned Paine into a pariah due to his sympathies for the French Revolution as well as his outspoken atheism. The rebellious Lippard engaged with Paine due to a resurgence of Paine's works as relevant source material for the labour movements of the 1830s and 1840s. Although, like most of their fellow Americans, Brown and Lippard held serious reservations about Paine's prominence, their Gothic tales retain a strong link to the Painite tradition. The radicality that Painites impressed upon the heart of American democracy lingers in the shadowy corners of their narratives.

At the same time, these two men, for reasons personal as well as political, could not outright endorse Paine's vision. Their narratives reflect an anti-Jacobin, counter-revolutionary tendency. 'Many authors [from this era] produced work possessed of some distinctively anti-Jacobin motifs and characteristic whilst manifesting an ideological ambivalence' (Grenby 2005: 204). It was easier for most early nineteenth-century writers to sell anti-Jacobin monsters to American readers than to endorse the ominous alternative. This market reality induced fictions replete with democracy's ostensibly grotesque horrors, even as writers like Brown and Lippard covertly, perhaps unconsciously, preserved the terrifying spectre of a radical democracy.

In short, the look and feel of the American Gothic offered fertile terrain on which writers could wrestle with the legacy of Paine as well as the future of his unorthodox vision for democracy. Ronald Paulson contends that modern democratic revolution proliferated as a political and aesthetic category. In turn, the American Gothic helped readers to imagine, or in certain cases fail to imagine, genuine revolution, as a 'phenomenon many believed to be outside their experience and accustomed vocabulary' (Paulson 1987: 1). In their sublime moments, authors like Brown and Lippard fostered a sense of awe at the notion of political upheaval, or the awe-inspiring restlessness at the heart of a true democracy. But the American Gothic simultaneously serviced the needs of an anti-Jacobin crowd by encouraging readers to experience dread at the thought of the revolutionary politics that was tearing France apart. The anti-Jacobins – the classification 'Jacobin' remained a necessarily plastic one – recycled conventional objects of horror, such as the libertine seducer, the charismatic spellbinder, and the blood-thirsty crowd, to repress signs of radical democratic intervention during the American Revolution, including mob protests and effigy burnings, and to promote the reactionary fears needed to superintend the expectations of what American democracy would become. The democratically minded antifederalists feared that 'the victorious federalists had abandoned the democratic impulse of 1776'; the conservative federalists, meanwhile, were 'fearful [of] mob role' (Burstein 2000: 147). As a result, 'fear of tyranny and fear of anarchy rent America in two' (187). Caught up in these cultural eddies, the Gothic works of Brown and Lippard prove to be 'object[s] and agent[s] of critique': they stir horror at the consequences of revolution even as they compel readers to experience internal as well as external revolutions through blind terror (McCann 1999: 110). In short, many American consumers of the Gothic have been too fearful of democracy and, at the same time, not yet fearful enough.

The Gothic novels of Brown and Lippard are therefore polysemous, or inherently contradictory. To understand better the fate of American democracy's radical dimension, I would like to tease apart the horrors and the terrors of these novels. Jerrold Hogle segregates horror Gothic (the confrontational, explicit, and gross) from terror Gothic, or that which 'holds characters and readers mostly in anxious suspense about threats [. . .] largely out of sight' (Hogle 2002: 3). Although it is never a simple one-to-one breakdown – Lippard, for instance, can be quite puerile in his descriptions of horrors associated with anti-democratic elites – I argue that, by and large, the *horrors* on display in texts by Brown and Lippard remain anti-Jacobin, however unaware the authors may have been of this fact. Many of the horrors in Gothic works by Brown and Lippard reflect the supposedly repulsive and reprehensible outcomes of the revolutionary energies boiling just beneath the surface in Pennsylvania. Concurrently, though, the *terrors* experienced in these books are frequently Jacobin in nature. For Brown and Lippard, faceless terrors, evoked through cliffs, caverns, trapdoors, and bottomless pits, sustain the imaginative work demanded of a radical democracy. That is, these literal and figurative openings preserve unexpected ruptures in the fabric of artistic as well as political experience. While horrors can be meticulously managed, terrors resist oversight. In this way, the ambivalent relationship of certain writers to their nation's evolving democratic project structured the formulaic patterns of the early American Gothic (and vice versa).

What is at stake for contemporary readers in bifurcating the Gothic works of Brown and Lippard between reactionary horror and progressive terror? To paraphrase Maximilien Robespierre, the most contorted of characters from the French Revolution, many defenders of democracy today are guilty of wanting a revolution without revolution. Self-described champions of democracy too readily accept a heavily orchestrated democratic experience and they do not dare to plunge into a real democratic revolution, with all of its attendant uncertainties. In his recent introduction to a collection of works by Robespierre, Slavoj Žižek contends that the subject must break away from what he calls a '(post)politics of fear' and take greater risks if they are to imagine a 'better world' (Žižek 2017: xxvii). To initiate a plunge of this magnitude means pushing past conventional horrors, meted out on a regular basis, in order to confront the unnerving potential of a fully actualised democracy. Žižek wonders, 'How are we to reinvent the Jacobin terror?' (xxiv). This emancipatory terror should unsettle patrollers of the status quo and, at the same time, re-politicise a democracy that has become entirely too regimented, too thoroughly choreographed. By cutting through reactionary monsters, citizens might experience the bone-chilling terror that remains a crucial first step to democratic revolution. Importantly, Žižek recognises 'the connotations of horror fiction' within his own efforts to rehabilitate Robespierre's legacy (xiv). Let us revisit, then, the horrors and terrors of Brown and Lippard in the name of reassessing American democracy as a nightmare – for worse or, just maybe, for better.

Woke

Following the controversial Jay Treaty of the mid-1790s, in which American leaders aligned the nation's interests with a conservative Great Britain instead of a revolutionary France, Charles Brockden Brown was swept up into the incendiary debates of his day: 'In the midst of a city [Philadelphia] once again smoldering with revolutionary politics, Brown's imagination was at work' (Kafer 2004: 109). Brown's 'intellectual and political heritage' was rooted in the French Revolution, although scholars continue to debate if Brown's fiction is, in the final tally, all that 'radical' (Verhoeven 2004: 8). Brown had by the year 1800 all but abandoned his youthful affection for radical democracy as his compositions started to strike a more reactionary tone. *Edgar Huntly* rehearses the divided perspective on the Painite tradition: on the one hand, *Huntly* expresses counter-revolutionary horrors tied to the prospect of a revolutionary form of democracy; on the other hand, Brown's text preserves a sense of terror that remains a prerequisite for radical democracies. By reading *Huntly* in these distinctive-yet-related aesthetic registers, readers can make sense of the conflicted nature of Brown's Gothicised politics. I want to complicate further the political categories that have heretofore been applied to Brown's corpus. As Philip Barnard and Stephen Shapiro note, 'Brown was not a centrist liberal, but neither was he a conservative or socialist radical' (Barnard and Shapiro 2022: 552).

To understand the intellectual underpinnings of Brown's Gothicised politics, I would first nod at William Godwin, the British radical whose work was openly revered by Brown. Brown once called Godwin's *Political Justice* his 'Oracle' (qtd. in Stocker 2019: 273). Like Paine, Godwin sought ontological ruptures that would fundamentally reorient society. Against a 'timid reverence for the decisions of our ancestors', and counter to retroactive inducements made on behalf of an established order, Godwin's radical democrat must face the terrors of a world as well as a subject that has been constitutionally undone: 'Better were a portion of turbulence and fluctuation, than that unwholesome calm which is a stranger to virtue' (Godwin 2013: 27, 263). Following in the footsteps of Godwin, Brown saw democracy as a truly unsettling proposition, one that must always terrify the American people if it is to endure. Mary Wollstonecraft, Godwin's partner and radical intellectual in her own right, found that petitions for more democracy did not go far enough because they left intact arbitrary restraints upon female subjects. Wollstonecraft wished 'to see exploded' the status quo – to instigate a rupture in the 'feudal tenures' that secured the foundation of society (Wollstonecraft 1988: 82). By undermining the 'nerveless limbs' of posterity, Wollstonecraft imagined a much more radical democracy (16). According to both Godwin and Wollstonecraft, once democracy becomes too calm, it becomes undesirable.

However, not unlike Godwin and Wollstonecraft, Brown remained wary of a fully unleashed anarchic principle. On this front, Brown revealed yet another debt to figures associated with the French Revolution: this time, to its most vociferous critic, the philosopher Edmund Burke. Although Brown shared in the egalitarian sensibilities of Paine and Godwin, he was disturbed by radical groups in Pennsylvania like the vigilante Paxton Boys who, in the 1760s, attacked indigenous communities due to the perceived failings of the state legislature. Brown understood well the need for Godwinian revolutionary terrors to unsettle people but he concurrently acknowledged the acute horrors expressed by counter-revolutionaries like President John Adams or the anti-Jacobin preacher Timothy Dwight.[7]

Readers must therefore attend to Brown as a Janus-faced writer. Conservative writers habitually utilised horror as a preventative tool ('to do X means to suffer'); unorthodox ruptures in the fabric of society struck the anti-Jacobin as revolting – a revolution of the senses, in the most gag-inducing fashion. As we shall see, Brown's *Edgar Huntly* anticipates as well as responds to perceived breakages in the social order with graphic scenes of blood and gore. At the same time, and frequently in the very same text, democratic revolution remains of necessity a terrifying business. How else would privileged elites, entrenched within their stagnant status quo, ever change their ways? *Huntly* thus oscillates between two poles of the political sensorium.

Huntly tells the tale of a young man named Edgar who wanders through the Pennsylvania wilderness and encounters a world he no longer understands. On one level, he confronts the horrors of a world in which power-hungry individuals (including, unconsciously, himself) improve their station through murderous means. On another level, he encounters the terrors of a world in which he no longer understands his own place, in which his own security has been undermined as he encounters forceful young men that challenge traditional laws of inheritance as well as the accompanying illusion of stability. Brown's characters regularly confront the uncomfortable fact that their perceived liberty is an illusion and they are actually entangled in the legacy of their ancestors. From the blood of a panther killed by its eponymous character's (Quaker) hand, to the edge of dizzying precipices and bottomless pits, *Huntly* conveys in equal measure the horrors and the terrors of democracy in early America.

The anti-Jacobin horrors of *Huntly* lead Brown's reader to anticipate, as well as to pass negative judgment upon, the possibility of unexpected attacks upon social norms. Edgar's first monstrous 'brother', Arthur Wiatte, proves spiteful and depraved. The brother of Edgar's would-be benefactress, Wiatte supposedly schemes to get a hold of his sister's inheritance. The reader learns that Wiatte previously participated in a mutiny. In Brown's day, mutinies had a specific political valence: 'Sailors were prime movers in the cycle of rebellion ... emboldened by a revolutionary heritage' (Linebaugh and Rediker 2013: 214–215). Known for his gambling and debauchery, Wiatte

---

[7] Concerning the French Revolution, Adams wrote that democracy's 'conflicting passions' will 'produce slanders and libels first, mobs and seditions next, and civil war, with all her hissing snakes, burning torches, and haggard horrors' (Adams 2004: 364).

calls to mind images of rebel sailors fraternizing in the so-called disorderly houses of Philadelphia's Hell Town. These imaginary sailors resemble agents of democratic revolution, ever defiant of the authorities that forced them into press-gangs. At the time of *Huntly*'s publication in the 1790s, the vanguard suppressed the role that mutinous sailors played in the American Revolution. Even Thomas Paine selectively omitted details about the mutiny that took place during his own time aboard *The Terrible*. Wiatte's eventual disappearance from Brown's story, then, can be read as a sign that the vanguard has taken control of the narrative and erased all signs of radicality. Edgar himself succumbs to this logic when he agrees that Wiatte is 'pure unadulterated evil', a grotesque figure meant to evoke horror in the reader (63). 'What might not be dreaded from the monstrous depravity of Wiatte?' the text asks. 'Against an evil like this, no legal provision has been made' (81).

Meanwhile, Edgar tries to understand the disappearance of another 'brother', Waldegrave. Brother Waldegrave teaches at the negro free school and embodies the abolitionist spirit of Philadelphia. Following a 'revolution [that] took place in his mind', Waldegrave adopts his creed with 'the fullness of conviction' and 'the upmost zeal' (132). He matches the common description of a Jacobin offered by American reactionaries: a zealot with too much conviction; a leveller with uncommon political ideas.

Finally, consider Edgar's spiritual brother Clithero. The indignant Clithero spends a good deal of the novel in pursuit of his own caretaker. Clithero's 'Irishness' marks Clithero from the start as a likely Jacobin. Anti-Jacobinism in the 1790s involved 'demonizing all things foreign', especially when it came to Irish immigrants, a group regularly accused of being closeted papists executing a covert plot against the United States (Cotlar 2014: 110). The Irishman Clithero's 'anarchy of thoughts and passions' moves Edgar to feel 'horror and shuddering' (Brown 1973: 111). Clithero is the supreme radical of *Huntly* in that he dares to hope for advancement and boldly declares a growing sense of entitlement. Clithero confesses, 'I was likely to construct a thirst of independence, and an impatience of subjection' (57). The novel eventually silences Clithero, just as it does Wiatte and Waldegrave before him. Edgar's master returns, assumes the position of Clithero's 'tyrant', and then drives Clithero back into the tumultuous waters from which he initially sprang (261). In order to declare everything 'safe and in ancient order' (222), Edgar must be retrained to experience horror at the thought of Clithero. 'Clithero is a maniac', he faithfully intones. 'Clithero is a madman' (258–260). Indoctrinated by the authorities, Edgar solidifies his alliance with counter-revolutionaries by accepting Clithero as the conventional stuff of anti-Jacobin nightmares. Revolutionary 'brothers' with radical ideas about what they deserve must be erased from the narrative.

Over the course of the novel, Edgar learns to suppress his initial radical impulses. He confronts, in the most famous scene of the novel, his untapped revolutionary strength when he meets a 'savage' panther and dispatches the beast with a tomahawk (128). Recycling imagery from the American Revolution, Edgar resembles an indigenous warrior, and Edgar's colonial neighbours subsequently mistake him for a native and attempt to kill him. Mirroring the participants in the Boston Tea Party, Edgar wears the guise of the local tribesman; fellow colonists consequently perceive him to be 'a maniac or a ruffian' (216). And then, like the fabled Queen Mab, a leader of native resistance, Edgar 'boldly' defies 'his oppressors' (252). But just as the revolutionary brothers are sequentially struck from the story, Edgar must eventually submit himself to a much more managed democratic experience and figuratively kill his own animalistic impulses.[8]

And yet, although it undoubtedly depends upon reactionary horrors, *Huntly* remains punctuated by significant moments of terror in which Brown's reader must, like an imaginary Jacobin, question the very ground upon which she stands. Throughout the novel, young men resist their position within a rigid hierarchy: Edgar realises that his financial hopes have been dashed by laws of rightful inheritance, and so he unconsciously enters into a bloody rampage in response to his feelings of societal impotence. In a related sense, *Huntly* is a novel about somnambulists and the disorientation the subject feels upon being woken from a deep slumber – a harried process that simulates the real-world experience of revolutionary upheaval. With its myriad pits and precipices, the romanticised landscape of Norwalk compels Brown's audience to consider, in a visceral fashion, the ruptures demanded by a radical democracy: 'To plunge into the darkest cavities, to ascend the most difficult heights, and approach the slippery and tremulous verge of the dizziest precipices' (46). Edgar unexpectedly awakens in a cavern at the precise moment that the establishment has cast his secure, well-endowed future into doubt. His own oppression at the hands of his almost feudal society catapults Edgar into 'dark and untried paths' (130). For Edgar, this shock 'outroot[s] prepossessions so inveterate'; he rethinks who he is at the most fundamental level imaginable (115). He enters the wilderness and moves away from his customary routes in order to reform his own subjectivity, which is to say, he undertakes a revolutionary flight of fancy to commence a 'passage into new forms, overleaping the bars of time and space' (218). In the midst of reactionary horrors, Brown's reader confronts literal as well as figurative holes in the narrative. These yawning chasms evoke genuine terror. What if the imagined ground of subjectivity was suddenly torn away, and the subject

---

[8] As such, *Huntly* might be read as a 'Federalist nightmare' (Tompkins 1986: 58).

was thrust into a place of abject uncertainty? As a Gothic writer, Brown strove to do nothing less than rewrite 'the conditions of political subjectivity in an Atlantic world' (Roberts 2014: 80).

When read through a bifurcated aesthetic lens of horror/terror, Brown's *Edgar Huntly* tracks how reactionaries repress the latent radicality of American democracy and how that latent radicality returns from its repression. Edgar feels 'outward shock' (horror) at the animalistic urges that animate his acquaintances as well as himself; at the same time, he undergoes an 'internal revolution' (terror) – a radical remaking of his subjectivity against an oppressive establishment that works to keep him in his 'proper' station (Brown 1973: 226). Brown's text reflects a society defined by the conventional horrors of the anti-Jacobins as well as the terrors that accompany true revolution.[9] If American readers long to live in a democracy worthy of its name, they should know how to tell the difference between these modalities.

'The Grotesque-Sublime'

Unlike Brown, whose political profile was rather opaque, George Lippard was an unapologetic radical democrat, a bloc known colloquially in his day as Loco-Focos. Lippard worked for a democratic law firm, published a weekly newsletter concerned with reformist issues, and founded The Brotherhood of the Union (a secret society that strove to advance the cause of the common labourer in Philadelphia). Crucially, Lippard saw in Brown a kindred spirit and dedicated a number of his works to his Pennsylvanian predecessor, including the Gothic novel that this section considers at length, *The Quaker City, Or the Monks of Monk Hall* (1845). *Quaker City* was the bestselling novel in the United States prior to the 1852 publication of Harriet Beecher Stowe's *Uncle Tom's Cabin*, and, perhaps surprisingly, given its mainstream acceptance, the text 'brims with radical democratic energies' (Emerson 2015: 107). This novel is a loose constellation of unsettling vignettes, held together by the barest of threads: a pair of star-crossed men battle over the fate of an innocent sister; the innocent sister is lured into Monk Hall, a den of sin in Philadelphia, and the majority of the book focuses upon attempts to rescue her from the talons of the city's wealthy villains. Lippard's book examines how the wealthy few commit covert crimes against the masses and, as such, it offers a stinging rebuke of Philadelphia's anti-democratic elements. Said another way, *Quaker* reproduces the soul-quaking terrors of a democratic revolution (or Terror, to sustain the era's Francophobilia/ Francophobia strains). In its most terrifying scenes, scenes in which the political

---

[9] Anthony Galluzzo surmises that Brown coded his narrators as unreliable to avoid the scrutiny of the counter-revolutionaries in power (Galluzzo 2009).

as well as aesthetic floor is quite literally pulled out from under character and reader alike, Lippard's *Quaker* holds open the promise – a threatening promise, certainly; a promise founded in requisite shocks to the system – of a radical democracy.

The 'specter of Jacobin conspiracy' stalks Lippard's seminal text (Cotlar 2014: 106). *Quaker* occasionally pivots from revolutionary terror to reactionary horror. Alexander Hamilton referred to the radicals of Pennsylvania as 'the Jacobin Scandal-Club', and this supposedly unflattering moniker resurfaced decades later in countless responses to the labour movements of the 1830s and 1840s in which Lippard participated. Counter-revolutionaries hunted down evidence of a widespread conspiracy among the revolutionaries espousing democratic change.

In what may have been an attempt to attract a broader audience, Lippard rehashed anti-Jacobin talking points by conjuring images of the grisly excesses of the Terror, including the massacres of 1792 as well as the public executions of Louis XVI and Marie Antoinette in 1793. Burke once described the French Revolution as 'a deformed, grotesque creature, more terrifying than any of the monsters which have overwhelmed and enslaved the human imagination' (qtd. in Tocqueville 2008: 20). Even that staunch defender of American democracy, Alexis de Tocqueville, shared some of Burke's apprehensions: 'No sooner did the head of this monster make its appearance, then its peculiar and terrifying character emerged . . . it undermined the foundations of society . . . the human mind looked upon it with open-mouthed disbelief' (Tocqueville 2008: 19). Echoing this fear-mongering, the most sensational aspects of *Quaker* support the value of orthodox family bonds. Lippard upheld the ideal of a traditional family against the assumed ideological zealotry of revisionists lurking in the pubs and club rooms of Philadelphia. His novel appealed to a conservative wing of American politics by exposing and then squelching revolutionary energies.

But readers should not forget that Lippard openly identified as a radical democrat, and so it would be misleading to dismiss the horrifying excesses of *Quaker* as proof positive that Lippard simply profited from an all-too-familiar Francophobia (feelings that had been percolating in America since before the XYZ Affair of 1797, during which Federalists seized upon anti-Jacobin imagery to consolidate their power). Things are much muddier than they appear.[10] For instance, secret societies play a complicated role throughout

---

[10] Lippard seconded Paine's assessment that the French Revolution was 'the first great effort of man to free himself . . . since the crucifixion'; at the same time, he rehashed monstrous imagery commonly used to describe the Reign of Terror, deeming it 'all that is grotesque, or terrible, loathsome' (Lippard 1894: 8–9).

the text. On the one hand, Lippard channelled the counter-revolutionary when he imagined Jacobins to be nefarious, conspiratorial, and utterly secretive. He used horror to attract a conservative reader that remained wary of radical democracy. On the other hand, Lippard founded his own secret society, and he recycled the populist musings of an Antimasonry movement that railed against a hidden cabal of monied elites. Indeed, popular democratic societies of that day 'looked to the [French] revolution for examples and solidarity' (Wilentz 2005: 53). Lippard evoked feelings of terror to evince a thorough rewiring of the American mind. These dual sensations reflect the ubiquity of literary conventions associated with anti-Jacobinism as well as the endurance of the Terror as a productive source of radical ideas in America. To illustrate this point, I now turn to three of the most conflicted elements of Lippard's novel: the pit, the dream, and the false prophet.

The French Revolution lingers in traces throughout Lippard's text. Readers learn that a 'wealthy foreigner' first erected the titular Monk Hall, with its 'mass of black and red brick' (Lippard 1995: 46). While it is improbable that Lippard would have been familiar with Stendhal's 1830 work, *The Red and the Black*, since it would not be translated into English for several decades, Lippard was unquestionably aware of the sartorial markers of the Bourbon Restoration – red for the revolutionary soldier, black for the conservative clergy – as well as the original Jacobin flag, with its red backdrop and prominent black lettering. With its colour-coded design, Monk Hall visibly connotes the revisionist energies that surged in revolutionary France. In similar ways, *Quaker* begins in an imposing Tower that calls to mind the Bastille in Paris, the storming of which helped to launch the French Revolution. Within this Tower, the tyrants of Philadelphia imprison innocent victims. Lippard explicitly marked many of the debaucherous occupants of Monk Hall as French: the villain Lorrimer is a libertine who wears 'a vest of plain white Marseilles' and drinks champagne, an identifiably French alcoholic beverage (89). Lippard's novel further underscores its villain's associations with the French by gesturing at a devilish seducer, Claude Mellnotte, from a play by Bulwer. Elsewhere, one of the 'fallen' women illustrates her fallenness by donning the 'silks of France' (249). Given Lippard's faith in radical democracy, why did he wed the Quaker City's den of sinfulness to caricatures of French radicalism?

One answer to this question may be found at the edge of a pit at the centre of Lippard's story. Beneath Monk Hall, readers discover an immeasurable chasm that elicits unspeakable terrors. The monstrous gatekeeper of Monk Hall, Devil-Bug, ventures to its brink, and although he laughs off the gruesome figures that slouch through the building, even he 'shudders' at the thought of the pit and the prospect of going down 'step by step into the lowest depth' (304–305). The pit of Monk Hall fills Devil-Bug 'with a feeling of supernatural awe' (229). The pit enabled Lippard to juxtapose the superficial horrors of Monk Hall with the more bone-chilling, foundational terror of the unknown. A strange object of terror as well as liberation, Lippard's pit provides a breath of fresh air in an otherwise toxic atmosphere. It is the only escape route through which victims might exit Monk Hall: 'The foul atmosphere of the Tower Room, lost half its deadly qualities [. . .] as the cool air, came rushing from the chasm' (122). Moreover, as the literal and figurative opening at the heart of the novel, the pit signifies the breach that is required as the basis of a radical democratic consciousness.[11] Because any radical democracy demands a lack of secure footing – the open-endedness of a society that can be perpetually made anew, similarly evoked in the wilderness of Brown's *Huntly* – Lippard's pit provides a sublime object of contemplation. Its terror is the salvation of the story because it is the only thing that can effectively unnerve the powerful despots shambling above.

Relatedly, Lippard made liberal use of unseen trapdoors, the presence of which routinely removes literal as well as figurative floors from beneath characters and readers. The horrors of Monk Hall pale in comparison to the abject terror of the unknown at its core: a terror made all the more palpable by the structure of the story as well as its titular edifice. The frontispiece to the first edition of *Quaker* visualises this terror by positioning the characters around a gap in a curtain that exposes an inky blackness, or the unknowable at the centre of Lippard's tale (**Figure 2**). The fissure of democratic open-endedness remains gaping beneath the floorboards of the status quo. Through his multiple, unexpected openings, Lippard generated a nightmare that opens always to an even worse nightmare: 'A terrible awakening' (544). For Lippard, it is only from such a state of heightened suspense that the vanguard could ever be substantively challenged.

This contrast between the horrors of the French Revolution, which trigger anti-Jacobin responses, and the awesome openings that terrify the elites appears again in Devil-Bug's apocalyptic dream. Devil-Bug's dream of the end of the world presents a two-faced portrait of 'the people' in the throes of revolution. On the one hand, the text shows 'throngs of laughing citizens', set off to attend the execution of a king and enact 'the vengeance of the People' (378, 347). On the other hand, Lippard's novel reveals a multitude of shrouded dead, marching unrecognised alongside their counterparts. The 'Monarch's

---

[11] I concur with Mary Unger's assessment that Lippard's spatial arrangements, his 'spatial deviance', undermine 'antidemocratic elitism' (Unger 2009: 20). The novel's many trapdoors and pits serve as aesthetic renderings of the ruptures required in a radical democracy.

Designed by Darley, for Lippard's Quaker City.

Figure 2 Readers glimpse a dark chasm at the centre of George
Lippard's Monk Hall

terror' strikes when the royal personage at last sees the unseen 'People' rising
up against him (390). In this way, *Quaker* forces its reader to gaze through two
prisms at once: to feel anti-Jacobin horror at the threat of a grotesque, anarchical mob and, at the same time, to feel Jacobin terror (the 'Monarch's terror',
to be precise) at the sudden recognition of a righteous People that had, until
that moment, remained invisible to him. Radical democracy shuttles readers
past their reactionary horrors to experience a terrible awakening in which what
had previously remained out of sight – a multitude comprised of common
laborers – bursts unexpectedly into view. To describe this odd admixture of
sensations, Lippard employed the term 'grotesque-sublime' (305).

    In closing, let us consider the doubled character of Signor Ravoni,
a tyrannical madman that appears at the close of *Quaker*. The ruthless demagogue places his listeners under a spell in an attempt to create a new world order.
Once more, Lippard coded his arch-villain as French, as Ravoni wears
the costume worn by 'the Chevaliers of France' prior to the French

Revolution (421).[12] This connection is made even more explicit when Ravoni declares, 'When the pikes of the Revolution glittered around the scaffold of a doomed King ... I was there!' (423). Moving parallel to the trajectory of Jacobin France, *Quaker* marches from the prison Tower of Monk Hall to Ravoni's Temple. Lippard's readers would have recalled how, following the Revolution, King Louis XVI awaited his execution in the Temple in Paris. An unsettling circularity materialises as Ravoni's Temple, like Monk Hall, contains 'all the horrors of the Bastile [sic]' (528). The anti-Jacobin horror of Ravoni is that he plays the part of spell-binder, a manipulator, a powerful populist; the Jacobin terror of Ravoni is that he signifies the chasm of an impending revolution, an apocalyptic upheaval of the old order in favour of 'a giant Truth' (424). Lippard encapsulated the tension between the horrifying and terrifying visages of Ravoni in a line that records the audience's initial reaction to Ravoni's spectacle alongside the compensatory reaction of his habituated crowd: 'The first awful pause of *terror* was past, and a murmured cry of *horror* shook the room' (441, emphasis mine). Although the Janus-faced Ravoni eventually elicits reactionary cries of horror at his gruesome deeds, the far greater danger might be the 'awful pause of terror' that accompanies his revolutionary threat. Before the reactionaries can repress them, radical democrats depend upon upsetting moments of rupture.

In his analysis of the Janus-faced Robespierre, who was both revolutionary and tyrant in one, Claude Lefort underlines the paramount value of the sublime within a revolutionary imagination. Lefort maintains that Robespierre effectively elicited fear among his followers that 'today's heroes may be tomorrow's guilty men', which is to say, a fear of the democratic imperative that a central seat of power is only ever temporarily occupied (Lefort 1988: 67). Robespierre intuited that a revolution would lose steam if it became terminable by erecting institutions that depend upon cultish reverence and an illusion of consensus. He understood all too well the revolutionary need for a lasting Terror, and so he tarried with 'an absolute gap' and cultivated 'a fascination with the abyss' (83–84). As we have seen, Lippard rendered visible Robespierre's absolute gap through his many textual trapdoors and yawning pits.

Lippard's Ravoni conjures the tortured figure of Robespierre. Like Robespierre, Ravoni is a clandestine antagonist and, from the vantage point of the anti-Jacobin at least, the horrifying figurehead of a vast conspiratorial movement. By all accounts, Robespierre, anticipating Ravoni, was a master of 'crowd manipulation' as well as a moral preacher with 'deep convictions',

---

[12] Another of Lippard's arch-villains, known as the Personage, summons images of 'those corrupt Ministers, who ruled the luxurious kings of France' (Lippard 1995: 549).

prone to sermonizing (Furet 1995: 148). Although Lippard's Ravoni is clearly a monster, he is a monster with whom Lippard would have partially identified. Mirroring Lippard's own secret society, the Brotherhood of Ravioni inverts the brotherhood of Monk Hall by signalling a new future, born from the ashes of a corrupt past. Ravoni and Robespierre are both 'execrated and exalted': they remain ever-shifting symbols, 'the protean specter of Jacobinism' as well as its active repression (Lippard 1995: 1, 189).

Readers can preserve the radicality of American democracy by preserving the terror at the heart of the early American Gothic. Beyond its reactionary horrors, the early American Gothic awakened its audiences in unknown caverns and goaded them into gamboling around bottomless pits, thereby opening themselves to the requisite ruptures of a real democracy. The Gothic works of Lippard and Brown illustrate how American democracy must terrify audiences to the very marrow of their being. While many Americans have been too frightened by the prospect of democracy, assuming reactionary or managerial postures, many Americans have not feared democracy enough for it to flourish fully. The readers who demand systemic changes are left waiting at the precipice, hungry for a better terror to come.

3 The Jacksonian Gothic

Together, American democracy and the American Gothic came of age. Andrew Jackson served from 1829 to 1837 as the nation's first populist president: a leader whose ostensibly democratic regime stirred incredible amounts of anxiety amongst the elites that had presided over the Era of Good Feelings, in which democratic engagement was quite limited. The surge of voter participation under Jackson, as well as Jackson's professed love of the so-called common man, signalled a monumental shift in governance (in theory, if not always in practice). Multiple Gothic writers cultivated literary terror alongside a burgeoning fear of Jacksonian democracy. In tales from prominent figures including Nathaniel Hawthorne, Edgar Allan Poe, and Herman Melville, Jackson's authoritarian democracy proves to be America's greatest nightmare. While it is relatively common to read the work of these writers as a sign of Americans being too fearful of democracy – and there is a kernel of truth to this assessment, given the differing degree of inegalitarian sentiments displayed by the authors in question – I would argue that these works more significantly signalled to their Jacksonian reader that she was not yet fearful enough.

It would be an error to cast these authors, or their respective audiences, as mere reactionaries engaged in a snobbish dismissal of an empowered electorate. After all, Jackson was a demagogue who exploited the pretence of democracy to exploit marginalised peoples and expand an oppressive economic system, all while proposing tyrannical initiatives like the censorship of mail.[13] The Whigs viewed their Jacksonian opponents as covert despots that practised subterfuge 'to create an empire of influence' (Wilentz 2005: 486). Political cartoonists of the time routinely depicted Jackson in this light (**Figure 3**).[14] For the Gothic figures in question, the fear of Jacksonian democracy was a fairly reasonable one, since Jackson's democratic triumphalism foreshadowed a dismal drift into despotism – from *E pluribus Unum* to *ex uno plures*, or from the will of Many to the will of One (and only One). 'Democracies carry within them, by their very nature, the prospect of their own totalitarian negation', Maurice Gauchet observes (Gauchet 2016: 183). Democracy appears to possess a latent 'will to sameness' (205). J.L. Talmon labels this phenomenon as *totalitarian democracy*, or 'a dictatorship based on ideology and the enthusiasm of the masses';

Figure 3 This widely circulated political cartoon portrays Andrew Jackson as an aspiring monarch

---

[13] Charles Wiltse writes, 'In four short years Jackson had led his party from bitter opposition to the 'consolidating' tendencies of John Quincy Adams to a form of authoritarianism that outdid even the Alien and Sedition Acts of Adams' father (Wiltse 1962: 65).

[14] This image can also be located, among other places, in Bernard F. Reilly (ed.), *American political prints, 1766–1876* (Boston, MA: G.K. Hall, 1991), entry 1833–4.

according to Talmon, the ideals of Jean-Jacques Rousseau, who played an invaluable role in the creation of modern democracy, helped certain actors to squash contradiction in the name of imagined unanimity and absolutist rule (Talmon 1970: 6). Some of America's earliest Gothic writers held that the Jackson regime heralded a romanticised equality that threatened to eradicate all signs of meaningful difference. But let us be a bit more granular: although scholarship concerning the American Gothic frequently handles 'the double' as a trope intimately tied to the personal psyche, Hawthorne, Poe, and Melville each revealed in their own way how the trope of the double can serve as a provocative political symbol of democracy's innate circularity. Paul Downes comments that these writers 'trouble simple solemnizations of democracy' by gesturing at 'the specific forms of terror and uncertainty introduced by post-feudal and egalitarian forms of social belonging [. . .] *a monstrous singularity*' (Downes 2004: 31, emphasis mine). Like Downes, I take seriously the fears that Hawthorne, Poe, and Melville expressed in regard to the Jacksonian democratic imperative – its monstrous singularity – that was consuming early nineteenth-century America.

To muse upon a circular democracy was not an uncommon practice during this era. Ralph Waldo Emerson's transcendental meditations conjoined the self-reliant, sovereign subject to a vast fraternal order. In his well-known essay 'Circles', Emerson employed the image of a growing circle to illustrate the endless expanse of human development via democratic progress. But he always looped back to a solitary individual whose greatness encompasses all: 'The extent to which this generation of circles, wheel without wheel, will go, depends on the force or truth of the individual soul' (Emerson 1983a: 404). 'Circles' closes with a citation from Oliver Cromwell, a man widely recognised as one of the fathers of modern democracy. Emerson later noted 'the beauty that all circular movement has', before offering a clear vision of democratic Oneness: 'There are the gods still sitting around him on their thrones, – they alone with him alone' (Emerson 1983b: 1105, 1124). Rousseau famously claimed that democracy could only realise itself in a nation of gods because only gods, with their innate equal standing, could bypass the hierarchies of human exist-ence. Although he privately expressed wariness regarding the democratic project, Emerson publicly supplemented Rousseau's thesis by imagining a nation of gods, seated in a circle, independent yet in a state of absolute solidarity. Commenting upon similar visions of a rounded democracy, Elias Canetti details how the symbol of the circle calls to mind the Athenian arena with its members of a crowd sitting in a wreath-like formation, mirrored: 'They all look alike and they all behave in a similar fashion [. . .] strangely homoge-neous' (Canetti 1984: 28). The Jacksonian Gothic responds to this circular formation by exposing a dread of this strange homogeneity: the latent horror of an acutely spherical democratic imaginary.

Hawthorne, Poe, and Melville each exposed Emerson's democratic circle to be a prison in which sovereignty masquerades as egalitarianism and transcendental unity proves to be more hell than heaven. For one, self-fashioned democrats welcomed any electoral outcome except the outcomes that they did not deem to be adequately 'democratic', thereby culling oppositional ideas from the start. A democratic majority circled the proverbial wagons and compelled members of the minority to join in or be forcibly ejected. Moreover, laws were constantly rewritten according to the majority's will, which left no room for anything beyond the tightly circumscribed parameters of the majority's political vision. In other words, Jacksonian democracy perpetually demolished its purportedly open-ended mode of governance and replaced it with a mode of governance that was always-already foreclosed. At the same time, and in a related way, democratic idealists tended to laud a person – and, by extension, a people – that remained completely self-determined. In effect, a democratic subject supposedly (re)generated herself without external influence: 'A people is a people before giving itself to a king' (Rousseau 2014: 171, 190). The ideal democratic subject, be it a people or a person, maintained a perversely circular relationship with itself. Expressing much more than a reactionary refutation of consensual governance, practitioners of the Jacksonian Gothic therefore challenged what they believed to be the facile assumptions held by democracy's most starry-eyed proponents.

Surrounded

Nathaniel Hawthorne considered himself to be a promoter of democracy and he served in government posts under Democratic administrations. However, his Gothic stories reflect a much murkier political outlook.[15] In 1849, Hawthorne's anti-democratic feelings boiled to the surface after he was removed from his post at the Salem Custom House in the wake of a local election. Hawthorne responded to his ousting by composing a vitriolic letter in which he called Salem voters 'Jack Cades' (Cade was a rebel leader in fifteenth-century England) and contrasted himself, 'an inoffensive man of letters', with a *demos* comprised of 'thick-skulled and no-hearted ruffians' (Hawthorne 2002: 134). Likewise, in Hawthorne's fiction, democracy, with its constant revolutions and cyclical usurpations, frequently comes across as a self-

---

[15] In this sense, Hawthorne was not unlike his fellow New England intellectuals, many of whom were 'democrats in their libraries and Whigs at the voting booths'. Like a number of his close friends, the self-fashioned Democrat Hawthorne may have been 'a Whig by instinct' (Schlesinger 1966: 62, 85).

perpetuating delusion. Many of his tales confront claustrophobic brotherhoods. Hawthorne's protagonists wind up mercifully alone: not indefatigable or God-like, as in Emerson's account, but broken with aspirations curtailed. As they (re) trace Hawthorne's darker circles, readers recognise the ugly underbelly of Jacksonian democracy. In the first circle, the *demos* envelopes the will of an individual into Rousseau's imagined general will; in the second circle, a democratic subject, who ostensibly remains free and equal, requires only her own sovereign authority to affirm her larger purpose in the world.

Consider, for instance, Chapter XI: 'The Arched Window' from *The House of the Seven Gables*. Hawthorne's melancholy observer watches as an immigrant boy with a barrel-organ cranks a mechanised scene on the street below. When the crank stops, the vivacious players have brought 'nothing finally to pass' (Hawthorne 2005: 116). Doubling the barrel-organ show, Hawthorne's text turns promptly to a political processional, a democratic event marked by the text as a 'fool's play'. Bewitched by the 'vast, homogenous spirit' of the democratic display, Hawthorne's observer must avoid the allure of total unity within the mob and restore a sense of detachment if he is to avoid being absorbed into the faceless crowd (118). For Hawthorne, democracy involves interminable rotations of the metaphorical crank – a circular movement that spins actors madly in place.

In 'Alice Doane's Appeal', a brother defends his sister's honour by murdering her suitor. The brother and the suitor reveal themselves to be doubles: 'The similarity of their dispositions made them like joint possessors of an individual nature' (Hawthorne 1883: 286). In the face of the suitor, the brother glimpses the uncanny horror of true equality, a shared sovereignty that renders his own entitlement claims over his sister mute. The story's attention then leaps across generations to address the miserable multitude that orchestrated the Salem witch trials. Doubling upon itself, Hawthorne's ill-fated *demos* possesses a 'universal heart', which then transforms into a 'universal madness' (293). Due to its assumed universality, Hawthorne's 'unreal throng' melts into an 'indistinguishable cloud', as the 'whole surrounding multitude' gathers and their shadowy visages 'circle round the hill-top' (294). With his doomed doubles and ever-circling crowds, Hawthorne unveiled the Gothic element of Jacksonian 'egalitarianism'. Hawthorne's vociferous crowds only ever want to find themselves; his characters, in turn, search in futility at the outermost rim of an ever-narrowing democratic sphere.

Hawthorne's Gothic story 'Young Goodman Brown' similarly dwells upon unsettling democratic circles. A young man wanders into the woods and feels immediately as though he is encircled by 'an unseen multitude' (Hawthorne 1987b: 66). When confronted by this 'loathful brotherhood', the young man realises that his society forces citizens into an 'awful harmony' (72–73). The villagers become One, forming a dreadful sphere into which Hawthorne's trembling initiate has no choice but to enter. The democratic levelling of society threatens the solitary Goodman Brown as the intermingling of the multitude compels Hawthorne's protagonist to retreat inward into existential isolation. With yet another turn of the metaphorical crank, Hawthorne's characters orbit around each other with greater velocity, tarrying with a frightening degree of sameness. The young man meets his older self as well as his father, who peer at him through a 'smoke wreath' (Hawthorne 1987b: 73). Generations circle back upon themselves in a cosmic wheel. How does this abject circular movement inform a reader's understanding of Jacksonian democracy? It bears repeating that democracy is a form of government that supposedly gives birth to itself. The democratic project theoretically involves 'a power that *gives itself* its own law' (Derrida 2005: 11, author's emphasis). Said another way, the democratic subject does not await orders from on high but generates her own orders from within. Hawthorne's young man encounters himself everywhere he goes as his past, present, and future merge into an anxiety-inducing composite. To save himself from this motionless revolution, this revolution in a self-same spot, and to admit a power much bigger than himself, Young Goodman Brown becomes estranged from his community.[16] Readers witness the oppressive wreath of the *demos*, a grotesquely annular sovereignty.

Perhaps Hawthorne's most full-throated denunciation of democracy as a circular phenomenon, though, remains his story 'My Kinsman, Major Molineux'. An adolescent named Robin wanders into the city to locate his British uncle Major Molineux (the French origins of his name concurrently conjure Jacobin spectres). Robin finds himself caught in a sinister web of plotting rioters and uncanny doubles. Once more, a young man is surrounded, as 'fiends [...] throng in mockery *round* some dead potentate' (Hawthorne 1987a: 12, 17, emphasis mine). The first circle encompasses a multitude of revolutionaries, feverish with the contagion of democratic overthrow, as they swarm Robin and his elder relative. Hawthorne's readers glimpse the frightful unity of a fulfilled democratic wish: an imagined Oneness surges through the brotherhood, reaching its peak with Robin's hysterical laughter at the sight of his tarred and feathered uncle. On multiple occasions, Hawthorne himself worried about being figuratively tarred and feathered by the public and falling prey to 'the grin of the multitude' (Hawthorne 2002: 136).

---

[16] Hawthorne's letters reveal a man who felt his kind should maintain 'a higher position', akin to 'the sanctity of the priesthood'; he considered the will of the people to be inherently wrong, and so the scorn of common man is, for Hawthorne, a 'laurel-crown'—an Athenian mark of distinction (Hawthorne 2002: 136, 144).

In 'Kinsman', a second, more individualised circle manifests when Robin meanders around the city, pacing up one side of the street and then looping back upon his earlier tracks. Hawthorne's story traces a self-enclosed, solipsistic sphere as the young man becomes the author of his own ascent rather than the beneficiary of aristocratic privilege. The story opens: 'The people looks with most jealous scrutiny to the exercise of power, which did not emanate from themselves' (Hawthorne 1987a: 3). Like his Shakespearean namesake, Robin loses his grip on reality as the colonial order erodes. Robin becomes increasingly disoriented due to an absence of coordinates from his British ancestors. He can no longer distinguish greater powers, such as God or the so-called natural aristocracy, from the power that emanates from within himself. As a newly anointed democratic subject, Robin generates his own sovereignty by pacing in feverish circles. It is a dreadful thing to make one's way without a father figure, the story claims, and so Robin's interior and exterior conflate into a disturbing grey. After all, what could exist beyond the self-determining consciousness of a democratic subject?

Another pregnant figure in the story is Major Molineux's housekeeper. His uncle's oft-sighted housekeeper attempts to entice Robin into entering his uncle's house. The most notable quality of the ominous housekeeper remains her scarlet petticoat, which Hawthorne's text describes as 'a hoop' as well as 'a balloon'. The story amplifies the impression of the skirt's roundness with its commentary upon how the housekeeper's face appears uniquely 'oval' (Hawthorne 1987a: 8). Hawthorne's tale repeatedly emphasises the circular quality of this devious woman. Her sartorial circularity calls to mind the infamous Petticoat Affair (1829–31), during which the wives of Jackson's cabinet ostracised Secretary of War John Eaton for his marriage to Peggy Eaton; Mrs. Eaton was reportedly cast out by elitist Washington insiders. Hawthorne published 'My Kinsman' in the year 1832, immediately on the heels of this highly publicised debacle. With her acutely spherical petticoat, Molineux's housekeeper can be read as a reminder of how Jacksonian democracy appears to be inclusive but, in truth, remains quite exclusionary. Hawthorne thus articulated a central paradox: even as America democratised, its 'latitude for public debate was closing' (Feller 1995: 199). The metaphorical petticoat, which appears to grant refuge to every wayward stranger, in truth veils an inhospitable inner sanctum, since the secretive rooms are claimed by a parochial mob. In this way, Hawthorne's tale juxtaposes the housekeeper's spherical 'hospitality' with the countless thresholds through which Robin is not permitted to pass. Although the fraternal circles that almost consume Robin seem to be a sign of democratic inclusivity, they actually demarcate a line between 'the people' (that powerful political fiction) and its sworn enemies.

Beneath a pretence of universality, Jacksonian democracy reveals itself to be innately tribal, which is to say, the stuff of Petticoat governments. Caught within as well as without the scarlet hoops of Jacksonian democracy, Robin maintains a tenuous hold on his precious individuality.

Like Diogenes the Cynic, drifting through ancient Athens in search of wisdom, Robin resists the unwholesome allure of a democratic circle: the faceless multitude that orbits him; the dangers of a totalizing self-sovereignty; the partisan petticoat falsely parading as social leveller. Based in part upon his own miserable experience in political appointments, Hawthorne remained a fatalist when it came to American politics. He professed a preference for British culture over 'the tyranny of public opinion', and he posited that the American public was little more than 'a herd of dolts and mean-spirited scoundrels' (Hawthorne 2002: 186, 252). In sum, Hawthorne's vision of democracy was a dark one. Importantly, though, Hawthorne did not simply attack democracy to endorse 'natural aristocracy' (although he did on occasion profess inegalitarian beliefs); rather, Hawthorne's Gothic tales alerted readers to the abject circularity of American democracy in a Jacksonian guise: the grotesque doubling of despot and *demos*.

Revolutions

Embroiled in the Jacksonian climate, Edgar Allan Poe harboured misgivings on the subject of democracy. He came of age in the world of Virginia elites and he held quite firmly throughout his life to a belief in 'natural aristocracy'. At its core, Poe's macabre fiction expresses sincere doubts about the capacity of a general populace to govern itself. Larzer Ziff summarises, 'Poe feared the mob' (Ziff 1981: 70). Poe frequently depicted social reformers as fanatics of one stripe or another, and, even more damningly, he exposed the tyrannical tendencies of a Democratic agenda, made most visible in the grotesque demagoguery of Jackson himself. A glance at pictures produced by one of his best-known illustrators, Arthur Rackham, affirms Poe's anti-democratic streak.[17] The image that accompanies Poe's 'Imp of the Perverse' (**Figure 4**), for instance, underscores how Poe's story mirrors the narrator's desire to 'plunge' into the 'abyss' with the narrator's desire to submit himself to the judgment of 'the crowd' (Poe 1935: 14). Poe's perverse imps, pictured on the left, find their echo in the unbridled energy of the *demos*. Elsewhere, the image that accompanies Poe's 'Hop-Frog' conveys both the result of a democratic revolution as

---

[17] All of the Rackham illustrations first appeared in *Poe's Tales of Mystery and Imagination: Reprint Edition* (London: George G. Harrap, 1935).

Figure 4 The imps that attempt to pull Edgar Allan Poe's narrator into the abyss
find their mirror image in the rabble

well as the shame of a crowd that has turned a blind eye to the fiendish
demagogue in its midst (**Figure 5**). Rackham's illustrations convey the mistrust
that Poe felt towards the idea that the American populace could ever truly
govern itself – the people (*demos*) wielding the power (*kratos*).

Still, it would be a mistake to read Poe as a dyed-in-the-wool reactionary. Poe
remained deeply engaged in the debates over democracy that were consuming
the Jacksonian age. To dismiss Poe's politics as 'conservative' is hardly suffi-
cient because he did not merely reject democracy in favour of aristocratic rule.
Poe found despotism and Jacksonian democracy to be synonyms, doubles,
a kind of self-perpetuating cycle. In his poem 'The Conqueror Worm', Poe
worried over how a powerful person might find himself stuck in the self-same
spot (a democratic crisis of the highest order).

Readers most readily locate the anti-democratic edge of Poe's works in his
satirical stories involving Jackson and his political progeny. 'King Pest' deflates

Figure 5 The faces of a Jacobin mob manifest upon the walls
of this Spanish prison

the sombre pomp of Jackson himself a.k.a. King Mob.[18] From 'The Man that was Used Up' to 'Four Beasts in One – the Homo-Camelopard', Poe spent his early career painting democratic engagement with what can be described as the broad brush of a political cartoonist. Reflecting a widespread disillusionment with government following the economic distress of 1837, as well as his own personal disillusionment following his inability to gain a plum political post within John Tyler's administration, Poe's fiction confirms its author's Whiggish tendencies. (Of note, the opportunist Poe likely believed that stories with a partisan bent would be more marketable in the increasingly partisan press of the 1830s and 1840s.) Simply put, Poe exposed the Gothic underpinnings of so-called democratic ideals being championed by the Jacksonians. To theorise Poe's nuanced vision of democracy in greater detail, this section considers his early story 'William Wilson' in conversation with his later tale 'The Pit and the Pendulum': two works with alliterative titles as well as plotlines that subtly echo

---

[18] See William Whipple 'Poe's Political Satire', *University of Texas Studies in English*, vol. 35 (1956), 81–95.

one another. 'Wilson' tells the tale of a man haunted by his double until his dying day, while 'Pit' details the unsettling torture of a prisoner by the Spanish Inquisition. In the suggestive doubling of these texts, that is, in their self-circling, Poe's readers glimpse a yawning abyss that Poe saw at the centre of America's democratic experiment, or what Monika Elbert has called 'the annihilation of the individual' (Elbert 1991: 26).

For Poe, the danger of democracy comes not from outside but from within. The trouble with democracy stems not from an excess of Otherness, a fear of diversity that readers might assume a self-fashioned aristocrat like Poe to hold, but from the eventual absence of any meaningful difference between individuals. In 'Mellonta Tauta', Poe determined: 'The same opinions come *round* in a circle among men' (Poe 1984b: 873, emphasis mine). Poe consistently argued that the levelling effect of democracy, which promises to create absolute equality across the multitude, leads to an erasure of difference and therefore pushes America towards the antithesis of its professed ideals: 'What is everybody's business is nobody's' (873). Poe thus tarried around an abject circularity in which the assumed expansion of freedom and equality espoused by Jacksonians leads to its very opposite – an increasingly circumscribed society, dictated by an ever-narrower subset of the population. Although he did not comment upon the political valence of this ominous shape, Harold Bloom described Poe's fictional universe as an 'apocalyptic circle' (Bloom 1985: 11). Indeed, Poe viewed American democracy not as an escape from the clutches of the tyrant but as a tightening of the tyrant's grip. He painted a grim portrait of 'a perverted form of sovereignty', underscoring 'the excesses of sovereign power [...] the tyranny of the One' that was taking hold under Jackson (Rodriguez 2016: 39). Here Poe's readers encounter the shadow of *kratos* within democracy: power of an all-consuming variety that ostensibly includes everyone and yet (this amounts to the same thing) winds up including virtually no one.

'Wilson' and 'Pit' confront the self-destructive tendencies of American democracy in a similar fashion. Each story begins by visualizing a sovereign authority. In 'Wilson', the narrator describes a teacher with 'robes so glossy and so clerically flowing, with wig so minutely powdered' (Poe 1984d: 339); in 'Pit', the narrator obsesses over 'the lips of the black-robed judges' and the 'sable draperies' of the courtroom (Poe 1984c: 491). Following this encounter with an awesome sovereign power, the two narrators pace their proverbial cages to measure out the enclosures within which they find themselves imprisoned. Each story tells of attempts by these two protagonists to escape from hierarchical arrangements. The narrator of 'Pit' feels festering within him 'the idea of revolution' and he clings to 'the hope that triumphs on the rack' (Poe 1984c: 491, 501). Meanwhile, from under the oppressive thumb of heavy-handed authoritarians, the narrator of 'Wilson' tries to establish himself as 'a single exception' (Poe 1984d: 341). Through his 'imperious' behaviour, he tries to become the law: to make the law for himself rather than remain bound by edicts from on high (341). Yet each of the tales conclude with the profound failure of its protagonist to become sovereign over himself. Far from a panacea, democracy's promise of self-sovereignty destroys Poe's twin narrators. Nineteenth-century readers might well have responded to this exposure of the dark underbelly of Jacksonian democracy with a perverse sense of nostalgia for the cage.

'Wilson' is a story about a man plagued throughout his life by his double: a Gothic theme that amplifies the circular nature of democracy (the sovereignty intrinsic to a democratic collective and the democratic subject's assumed sovereignty over herself). Although he longs to control others, from his parents to his competitors, the narrator of 'Wilson' cannot shake the dread of 'equality' that his double represents (Poe 1984d: 342). When sovereignty is shared by all, the results are damning. Equality becomes a horrifying conceit, an all-consuming schema in which the will of a particular group, or a single subject, subsumes the will of everyone else. In this way, Poe effectively channelled 'the Whig fear of democracy's becoming authoritarian [and] submerging all into the mob by erasing differences' (Britt 1995: 202). Regardless of the narrator's presumed autonomy – he is, after all, the offspring of his own will, or will-son – and unmoved by his claim that he will 'submit not longer to be enslaved', Wilson's double holds illimitable dominion over him (Poe 1984d: 354). The double's 'inscrutable tyranny' blankets the relationship of the two men and so, when the narrator at last murders his double, the narrator effectively commits suicide (355). In much of Poe's fiction, the levelling effect of democracy produces a disturbing negation of difference.

Poe's vision of democracy leaves little room for individualism. The narrator of 'Wilson' tries to free himself from the bothersome equality that his double assumes by attempting to 'hesitate' and 'resist' (Poe 1984d: 355). But Poe's tale quickly neutralises the narrator's effort: when attacked, the double 'hesitates but for an instant' and reveals himself to be 'unresisting' (356). This dark equilibrium – a hesitation undone by its opposite; a resistance undermined by acquiescence – exposes a democratic impetus that leaves no room for the unexpected. Everything has always-already been calculated in advance. To employ one of Poe's favourite metaphors, the promise of democratic release reveals itself to be but a dream within a dream: 'Total equality is not a liberating ideal but a prison house' (Faherty 2005: 9).

Jacques Derrida returned to this monstrous singularity almost two hundred years later. Speaking out against the hegemonic initiatives of the United States in the Middle East being advanced in the name of democracy, Derrida wonders if American democracy only ever induces a solipsistic circle. Derrida echoes Poe when he equates democracy with the rack: a torture device that involves 'an encircling violence and an insistent repetition' (Derrida 2005: 8). For Derrida, this sort of democracy – the type once advocated by Jacksonians – trains a society to consider itself as both cause and effect, without externalities: 'God, circle, volt, revolution, torture ... a circular and specular autoaffection' (Derrida 2005: 14–15). Once the precepts of American-style democracy have spread into every corner of the globe, what is left of the plurality, the sense of difference, that theoretically drives a democratic project? Having announced its triumph as global consensus, American democracy leaves virtually no alternatives to itself, and so it forecloses the open-endedness that has been its *raison d'etre*. Forecasting figures like Derrida, Poe viewed democracy as a potentially torturous feedback loop.

Opening with a reference to Jacobin Houses, the hotbed of French democracy at the close of the eighteenth century, Poe's 'Pit and the Pendulum' offers yet another narrative about democratic 'revolutions'. The text describes the narrator's narrow evasion of an ever-descending pendulum as rats flood into the cell to gnaw off the robes that hold him. Rats serve as a metaphor for the Jacobin crowd that triggered the French Revolution. Rackham's illustration of the story captures the correlation between the faces of the Jacobin mob and the walls of the prison, thus underscoring Poe's suggestion that Jacksonian democracy has become a self-enclosed prison (**Figure 6**). The ravenous animals boldly move upon the narrator, thronging like a mass of 'fresh troops' (Poe 1984c: 503). They 'overrun' the barricades, foreshadowing the destruction of the prison that ends the story: 'My deliverers' (503). Calling to mind the storming of the Bastille in July of 1789, Poe's story creates a palpable sense of revulsion at the notion of a revolutionary mob. By marking the narrator's 'deliverance' in a heavily ironic fashion, Poe's tale implies that an assumed democratic escape from authoritarians is only ever a deeper form of imprisonment. General Lasalle grabs the swooning narrator at the last possible moment – but, as the wheel takes one more ominous turn, Poe's reader would have known all too well how, historically speaking, the Jacobin insurrection eventually became a Reign of Terror. The pendulum doubles as a guillotine, and the beheading of one French tyrant (Louis XVI) is followed by the beheading of another (Robespierre). In effect, the French Revolution and its aftermath exposed that the end of one sovereign is really just the assertion of a more absolute sovereignty. And this repetition, enacted under the banner of democracy, has left fewer and fewer resources for hesitation or resistance.

Poe's 'Pit' insists that Americans cannot rid democracy of its intrinsic *kratos*, or its latent hunger for imperial power. Poe here pondered over 'the undecidable limit between the demagogic and the democratic' (Derrida 2005: 67). Again,

Figure 6 The unruly crowd is disgusted, at last, by what its
demagogue has done

Jackson was an anxiety-inducing example of this abject circularity because he
famously 'liberated' the common people in order to enhance his own sovereignty,
which is to say, Jackson's ever-expanding enfranchisement of the common man
was accompanied by a frightening exclusion of dissenting individuals. Consider
the similar ways that 'Pit' closes in upon itself: its flattening of history, in which
disparate events, the Spanish Inquisition and the French Revolution, become
synonyms; its monomania, in which a single consciousness (the narrator's tyrannical 'I') eradicates everything exterior to itself. Recalling Hawthorne's Robin,
everything that occurs in 'Pit' may be a manifestation of the lone narrator's
unconscious. Poe's democracy therefore remains frightfully self-enclosed and
utterly circular. The reader must entertain 'the idea of revolution – perhaps from
its association in fancy with the burr of a mill wheel' (Poe 1984c: 491).

The horrors of the mill wheel manifest as a torturous repetition throughout
Poe's corpus. Poe worried about the rallying cry of an ostensibly democratic
regime that would marshal its subjects into a grotesque sameness, or what he

called 'an omni-prevalent Democracy' (Poe 1984a: 451). Like Derrida in the century to come, Poe conflated his assault on the tyrannical notion of reason with his attack on an omni-prevalent Jacksonian democracy. When brought to their limit, both reason and democracy abolish self-critique, as the touted transcendental Oneness of reason and democracy eventually overwhelms the operative capacity of these ideals to sustain a healthy degree of difference. As reason becomes instrumental, and democracy becomes a disguise for dominion, Poe's Gothic circles expose Jacksonian democracy's tendency to totalise. Just as Poe revealed that reason always blurs with madness, he illustrated how democracy invariably doubles as despotism. In turn, Poe discovered innovative ways to show that 'life on earth is not a closed circle' (Talmon 1970: 10).

Fraternity

According to Poe and Hawthorne, the Jacksonians were not yet afraid of democracy enough because they remained latched to the illusion of a comfortable consensus, or the circular homogeneity embodied in the populist ringleader Jackson. Like Poe and Hawthorne, Herman Melville feared that the bumptious Jacksonians wielded the instrument of democracy to silence their critics. At the same time, Poe and Hawthorne remained arguably too afraid of democracy because it threatened their own sense of entitlement, and so it can be said that they were too enthralled with their own projected horrors as well as too avoidant of democracy's productive terrors, that is, its requisite uncertainties. Unlike Poe and Hawthorne, Melville did not slide into an inegalitarian worldview; instead, his most Gothic works held that a radical democracy could create a fecund sense of terror to shock all-too-comfortable Democrats into facing the egalitarian premise at the heart of their own political project.[19]

One of Melville's most Gothic stories remains one of his most nuanced meditations on the subject of American democracy. *Benito Cereno* opens with the American captain Amasa Delano boarding a slave transport ship named the *San Dominick*, which is, unbeknownst to Delano, covertly under the control of rebellious slaves. Delano meets the dethroned captain Don Cereno as well as his ostensibly obedient slave Babo. After a prolonged visit, Delano learns that the slaves have risen to the status of masters and the colonial establishment summarily squashes the rebellion. Following in the footsteps of Hawthorne and Poe, Melville endowed his story with a distinctive uncanniness. Unlike the stories of Poe or Hawthorne, however, Melville's tale exposes the blind spots of

---

[19] Dennis Berthold argues that Melville sought a balance to avoid 'too much democracy as well as too little' (Berthold 2006: 161).

paternalistic Jacksonians by conjuring the spectre of a genuinely inclusive democratic vision.

Melville's *Benito* traces the circularity of Delano's supposedly democratic perception, which the story eventually unveils to be an innate narcissism. Because Delano can only ever imagine a world made in his own image, he simply cannot fathom that a slave like Babo would be shrewd enough to overthrow his captors. Delano believes that, in giving the slaves the benefit of the doubt and remaining wary of the ostensibly tyrannical Don Cereno, he is being a good democrat. Delano cannot comprehend Babo as an autonomous individual that could exist beyond his benevolent oversight, and so the captain mistakes his own delusional sovereignty for a type of egalitarian sentiment. The circular movements that comprise *Benito* offer a Gothic rejoinder to utopian visions of democracy.

The democratic circularity of Melville's story is made legible in the name of the vessel. The monicker San Dominick conjures several fantastical images: the island of Dominique, with its well-organised ethnic African majority and its perpetually threatened colonial planters; Saint Dominic, whose name was apocryphally uttered by agents of the Spanish Inquisition (the name of a gracious saint thinly disguised a craven pursuit of greater power by a select group). Echoing Poe's 'Pit', then, Melville conflates French and Spanish iconography to undermine the tenets of an oppressive Jacksonian democracy. The name San Dominick exposes Jacksonian democracy to be only ever a push for sovereign control. Whether he is likened to the supposed gift of democracy bestowed by the British upon the colonised peoples of Dominique, or to the exploitation of a saint's name to gain the upper hand over disenfranchised individuals, Delano remains more concerned with *kratos* (power) than *demos* (the people). The word Dominic, after all, shares a common Latin root with democracy as well as dominion (*dominus*).

By attacking the hypocrisy of widespread enslavement within a self-proclaimed democracy, Melville exposed an enclosed circle that allowed Delano to assume his position of absolute mastery under the guise of universal good will. The Gothicism of *Benito Cereno* remains tied to a persistent repression: unwilling, or unable, to confront genuine difference, or the possibility that something could happen that did not always-already confirm his existing worldview, Delano rests relatively easy in his authoritative role. Posing as a white saviour that gives slaves the benefit of the doubt, his apparent generosity only confirms his existing biases – a narrow self-reflection; an endless loop. Because Delano's 'democratic vista retains yawning blind spots', the captain exemplifies 'the blind stupidity of an American democrat' (Mihic 2014: n.p.). Melville drew ominous circles within Delano's psyche: 'Ah, these currents spin one's head round' (Melville 2001: 60). The entire tale proves to be a hermeneutic circle akin to the slave's padlock and the master's key: 'Significant symbols, truly' (51). In its final pages, the story reveals that the preceding work has been the testimonial of a privileged white man. Because Babo will not be deposed, Delano's perspective serves as the padlock that secures meaning as well as the key with which to unlock any interpretation of the preceding events. What passes as 'democratic' proves to be horrifically totalizing as the legal testimonies of white authoritarians secure a grim self-enclosure. History is written by the victors, and Delano's 'democratic vista' ultimately leaves Babo voiceless in the telling of his own story. The 'fraternal unreserve' that materialises between Delano and a fellow officious captain at the close of *Benito* can only be described as 'free and equal' due to the detachment of the two men from their maligned crews (100). The hermeneutical circle of democracy thus hides a tyrannical agenda as the climactic victory of the twin captains reveals itself to be the antithesis of Delano's professed aims. In a related sense, Derrida has shown how the term 'fraternity', greatly amplified during the French Revolution, actually disguises a set of oppressive gendered assumptions since the term 'fraternity' privileges male bonds as well as particular patriarchal perspectives on issues of inheritance and citizenship. Jacksonian democracy remains inherently despotic.

Melville forced his readers to share in the uncomfortable gaze of a paternalistic democrat. Delano watches as the ship's rabble blends into a fraternal circle and threatens the hierarchical coordinates by which Delano has long steered his private course.[20] Delano's horror underscores the significance of the name Babo, which may have signalled to Melville's audience the term *Babouvism*: a nineteenth-century French dogma that advocated absolute equality. When Delano sees family enclaves of slaves, he observes, with clinical dehumanisation, that the groups move like bats in large orbits, or 'social circles' (Melville 2001: 68). What is to be made of these fraternal circles created by the crew members of the San Dominick? Readers might recall common cultural attitudes towards mutinous sailors and slaves in early American life. Peter Linebaugh and Marcus Rediker demonstrate how the motley crew, commonly referenced at the time as a many-headed hydra, struck fear in the heart of the established order because it represented a radical democratic shift. The motley crew, 'an organized gang of workers', paralleled the revolutionary crowd, and it was fundamentally 'multiethnic as well as independent of leadership from

---

[20] An observer of Jackson's inauguration remarks upon a sense of intense fraternal enclosure from which elites were potentially being excluded: '*The Majesty of the People* had disappeared, and a rabble, a mob, of boys, negros, women, children, scrambling, fighting, romping. What a pity what a pity!' (Smith 1906: 293–294, author's emphasis).

above' (Linebaugh and Rediker 2013: 212–213). The slave and the sailor forge a 'broader social form of cooperation' (213). Tales of motley crews regularly injected a radical democratic sensibility into the national discourse as newspapers recounted the revolutionary victories of piratical enclaves. Sailors would sometimes don black face to protest their oppression, as in the protests against the Stamp Act, while slaves would occasionally whiten their faces to defy their mistreatment. This masquerade of doubles adds yet another layer to Melville's Gothic narrative because the real trepidation for pseudo-democrats like Delano is the terror of a true egalitarian fraternity. Compelled to occupy Delano's claustrophobic perspective, Melville's reader senses a swirling mass that threatens to erode every sign of difference.

Melville forced his reader to share in Delano's dread of an encroaching hybridisation of sailor and slave: 'A clamorous throng of whites and blacks ... in one language, and as with one voice, all poured out a common tale of suffering' (Melville 2001: 38). Unsettled by the 'strange crowd' that surrounds him, Delano worries about 'the indiscriminate multitude, white and black' (56). In the climactic scene of *Benito*, sailors and slaves alike leap into the sea in a frenzy of intermingling cries, and Delano finds himself suddenly confounded by his own inability to distinguish friend from enemy. Devoid of captains, the motley rebels form a ring around the ship, 'helplessly mixed' in a pervasive greyness (86).[21] Delano struggles to maintain his bearings as the hierarchy of race ceases to function and he subsequently stares into the void of a levelled society. In one pregnant moment, an old sailor, the embodiment of familiar docility for Delano, fades into the masses: 'In the crowd he disappeared' (64). Elsewhere, the mess hall aboard the *San Dominick* transforms into a horrifying mess as Delano surveys 'whites and blacks singing at the tackle ... mouthfuls all around were given alike to whites and blacks' (67).[22] This moment echoes a well-known moment from Chapter 94 in Melville's epic *Moby-Dick*, 'A Squeeze of the Hand', in which sailors indulgently join their hands together to make manifest the promise of *E Pluribus Unum*, or One out of Many. A fraternal wreath encircles sailor and slave alike. With his own

---

[21] Harkening back to Poe's 'Pit', Melville likened the revolutionary crowd to rodents in his more conservative poetry. In 'The House-Top', Melville wrote: 'The town is taken by its rats – ship-rats / and rats of the wharves'. The tumult of the riotous rabble eventually stirs up 'a mixed surf' (qtd. in Dillingham 2008: 136–137). He affirmed this sentiment in the sketch 'Charles Isle and the Dog-King', in which piratical characters overthrow a savage monarch and reveal themselves to be just as barbaric: 'Nay, it was no democracy at all, but a permanent *Riotocracy*, which gloried in having no law but lawlessness' (Melville 1984: 791, author's emphasis). While Melville did resist certain corrupt forms of democracy, he never relented in his faith in its utopian possibilities.

[22] Robert K. Martin highlights the importance of friendship in Melville's work: 'The brother-bond forms a circle, a sacred sign of unity that cannot be broken' (Martin 1986: 66).

latent superiority in jeopardy, egalitarianism encircles Delano like a monster from the deep.

The real terror of *Benito Cereno*, then, is the concept of a democratic fraternity freed from its covert racialised dominion (one might think, here, of Jackson's genocidal attitudes towards indigenous peoples). Can one sever two of the roots of Dominick: democracy from dominion? Relatedly, self-sovereign thoughts plague Jacksonian democrats like Delano, 'turning over and over' in a circular fashion, as they barricade themselves from the viewpoints of excluded individuals such as the mutinous Babo (Melville 2001: 65). Through its tracing of these claustrophobic circles, Melville's *Benito Cereno* gestures at the outermost perimeter of its democratic enclosures – the exterior of fraternal circles; the destabilisation that would accompany a good faith campaign for equality. By facing down the hypocrisy of American racism in its democratic guise, Melville went farther than either Hawthorne or Poe as he sought to re-open American democracy. Daniel Malachuk argues, 'Melville was committed to the principle of equality, not the instrument of democracy' (Malachuk 2021: 147). That is, Melville imagined the principle of democracy as something much more powerful than a narrowly circumscribed Jacksonian instrument; he viewed democracy as a principled mode of governance that could empower readers to imagine something beyond the cramped confines of the Democrat's private as well as public life. Melville therefore gestured at new political horizons through his terrifying democratic vistas. He showed that the American Gothic has the potential to expose audiences to the *requisite* fears of democracy. These audiences might in turn confront their own reactionary horrors – not to bury them with too much haste but to mature beyond them as responsible citizens.

In closing, the Gothic circles of Hawthorne, Poe, and Melville reflect the perils of Jacksonian democracy. Their concentric circling of *kratos* (power) with *demos* (the people) could incite in American readers, then as well as now, a repulsion regarding their purportedly democratic system. But as Melville's *Benito Cereno* demonstrates, the nature of this fear, 'the soulless terrors of Jacksonian Democracy', should not be cast as the mere stuff of nightmares, perpetuated by staunch reactionaries (Faherty 2005: 18). These Gothic writers channelled a reasonable anxiety that American democracy was striving towards the antithesis of its stated aims. In their eyes, the young nation appeared to be building a democracy 'driven to domination' (DuFord 2022: 138). The spectres of the Jacksonian Gothic lurk beyond the outermost rim, taunting and tantalizing claustrophobic subjects with a world outside of their own – a democracy that has ceased revolving in its selfsame spot.

4 Spectres of Democracy

Upon first glance, the works of Shirley Jackson and Stephen King focus upon the mysterious engine that drives communities together or tears them apart. Consider Eleanor's precarious familial group in Jackson's *The Haunting of Hill House* (1959) or the slippery (re)alignments of the Losers' Club in King's *IT* (1986). Jackson and King each underscore the combustible engine of a democracy that compels small-minded people to form violent groups. But upon second glance, the political visions of Jackson and King prove to be inverted images of one another: because of her uneasy alignment with the gentry class, made legible in her fiction via a healthy dose of irony as well as apocalyptic dread, Jackson left the fate of American democracy decidedly uncertain; in contrast, King's democracy leads always to demagoguery and destruction. The distinction really matters. Whereas Jackson's lack of assurance about democracy affirmed one of democracy's core truths – specifically, its requisite open-endedness – King's pessimistic certitude about mob rule serves as a harbinger of American democracy's imminent demise.

Democracy haunts American life. It is both everywhere and nowhere at once. But let us be more specific when detailing the contours of this haunting: democracy is 'a continuous process of egalitarian inclusion and power sharing made possible by tireless agitators' (Taylor 2019: 5). In effect, democracy involves an unending state of restlessness. A democratic people can never fully realise their aims because their political demands as well as alliances remain forever mutable. A truly democratic society never achieves stasis because stasis requires the termination of what needs to be a continuous process. Simply put, a democracy devoid of uncertainty would no longer be democratic, at least not in any meaningful sense. Democracy therefore endures as the most prominent of America's political spectres: 'An elusive fantasy, forever out of reach, forever unrealized' (Miller 2018: 131). Political theorists including Claude Lefort, Joan Copjec, and Chantal Mouffe have shown how democracy persists as an immaterial presence. With a propensity for the unseen, as well as an appetite for that which agitates, the American Gothic offers an ideal site for grappling with democracy as an immaterial presence. And just as the American Gothic often works best when its monsters do not take a visible form but instead dwell in the ephemeral realm, in a shadowy substrate that defies description, American democracy works best when it maintains a somewhat shapeless quality.

For her part, Jackson depicted the patrician world in which she lived as a cloistered fantasy world. Yet beyond the horizons of her aristocratic, agoraphobic universe, something else abides. Even as Jackson's elitist characters ostensibly borrow the grammar of the horror novel to reject the *demos* (the democratic populace), the imminent threat of a world without hierarchy invariably returns from its repression. To Jackson's plutocrats, the egalitarian threat remains incomprehensible and thoroughly unnerving. King, meanwhile, endows democracy with the tangible and invariably repellent form of the despot. He expresses this ungodly bond between the *demos* and the despot in his tome *The Stand*: 'Let the princes of this world get along as best they could with the people who had elected them . . . they deserved each other' (King 1991: 51).While Jackson's anti-democratic façade fosters democratic desires, King's works fuel anti-democratic yearning as they reveal tyranny to be the preordained conclusion of a dead-end democratic experiment. Contrasting these distinctive visions, readers can recognise how the American Gothic preserves democracy best by refusing to exorcise democracy's amorphous phantoms.

Razing Demos

Shirley Jackson's texts track wealthy Americans as they shirk their democratic responsibilities. Her elites cling to illusions of independence by sealing themselves off in hermetically sealed castles and stubbornly refusing a democratic charter. Some critics have read Jackson herself as a closeted reactionary; after all, she was the child of a privileged caste and the wife of a college professor at a highly selective liberal arts institution. However, by making the term 'democracy' synonymous with the unrealisable, which is to say, as the sublime object at the centre of her fictionalised New England villages, Jackson not only rendered the levelling potential of democracy as that which terrifies her reader but – this point remains essential – she also upheld democracy as that which remains the most *real* for her reader. Due to their need for the illusion of hierarchy, members of Jackson's gentry imagine the masses in the form of comforting horrors: conventional bogeys that mask the underlying fear of a lost social order. In turn, the true terror of these tales never fully emerges, instead skulking ominously in the margins. Put simply, it is the terror of a universal equality. Jackson's Gothic stories tarry around the failure of American democracy to materialise and, by so doing, these stories maintain democracy as an impossible-yet-immanent promise.[23]

Admittedly, to render the threat of democracy as a loadbearing pillar of Jackson's fiction is to read against the grain. Biographers typically present Jackson as being apolitical at best. 'Her political knowledge was almost nonexistent', Judy Oppenheimer opines. 'Her vision was personal, not political'

---

[23] Slavoj Žižek argues, 'We can save democracy only by taking into account its radical impossibility' (Žižek 2009: xxix, author's emphasis).

(Oppenheimer 1989: 131, 164). In truth, Jackson dallied with Marxism during her college years and she was intensely self-aware when it came to feelings of chosen-ness among the American aristocrats with whom her family associated. A number of her stories skewer the upper crust by exposing their insecurities and lamenting their belief in their own superiority. At the same time, Jackson clearly wanted her reader to identify with the upper crust, however temporarily, and as a result her fiction transforms the democratic populace into a demonic force, a mobocracy that should not be allowed to govern itself. Jackson would have understood that paranoid perspective all too well since she felt set apart from her neighbours in the Green Mountain state and worried constantly about the power of groupthink, a residual concern in part held over from the atrocities of the Second World War. (King will swim in similar waters as a dissident forged in the fires of war in Vietnam.) Upon first glance, then, her narratives depict the rabble as a hellish brood that attacks any sign of difference, thereby reflecting midcentury America's fear of the *demos*.

Jackson's most famous story 'The Lottery' seemingly affirms Jackson's antipathy for the *demos*. The narrative depicts the gruesome native ritual of a small-minded village in which members of the tribe must draw lots and, if they are selected, the villagers stone them to death. In one reading, 'The Lottery' exposes the perversity of direct democracy when it likens casting lots to casting stones. Eligible members of the ancient Athenian *demos* selected their governing officials through the drawing of lots, in a process known as sortition. This procedure, which remained random by design, aimed to keep the pool of possible leaders fresh and thus avoid corruption. Anyone (or, almost anyone) could be chosen to lead. In 'The Lottery', direct democracy ostensibly permits the people to make their own decisions and instigate their own ruin. Jackson's fable appears to chastise the *demos* for behaving like a bunch of reckless children: 'The feeling of liberty sat uneasily on most of them' (Jackson 1991a: 291). When at last the villagers descend upon their innocent victim, they taunt her: 'Be a good sport ... all of us took the same chance' (298). It remains difficult not to interpret 'The Lottery' as proof positive of the tyranny of the majority. The story appears to underscore an anti-democratic need to protect elite individuals from irrational *doxa* (or, the vagaries of public opinion). In a letter to her agent, Jackson once slyly suggested: 'I got a letter from a lady saying didn't I once write a letter about an election where one of the candidates got killed with a rock? Did I, do you think?' (Jackson 2022: 225).

And yet Jackson never fully committed to such a fetishised vision of democracy. There are actually two levels in 'The Lottery' – the horrifying and the terrifying. As we have seen, at the first level, the reader shares the victim's reactionary horror when it comes to groupthink. At the second level, though,

Jackson's reader shares the terror of Old Man Warner, an aged member of the community troubled by the prospect of a populace that no longer holds onto its ritualised acts of violence. By inviting her reader to share in Old Man Warner's perspective, Jackson concurrently invited her reader to imagine the terrifying potential of a democracy that could live up to its own ideals. Like Old Man Warner, the reader might feel disquieted by the notion of a democratic society in which citizens would draw lots not to vilify one another but to expand participation and share in the collective work of forming a better society. If levellers did somehow usher in a democratic future, what would happen to the brutal antagonisms upon which Old Man Warner's way of life depends? Unsettled by the suggestion of a world without the comfortable horrors of prejudicial monsters, Jackson's Gothic works preserve democracy as a kernel of the sublime: a terror looming just beyond the borders of tightly cloistered communities, one that subverts the established norms of reactionaries like Warner.

Put differently, the horrific monsters conjured on behalf of class warfare actually *protect* Jackson's short-sighted characters (as well as her short-sighted audience) from what could be a genuinely egalitarian politics. Jackson's stories demonstrate how a visible struggle between aristocrats and 'the people' provides a degree of succour at the brink of an unspeakable terror – the loss of hierarchy that would accompany a full-fledged democratic turn. One cannot too quickly dismiss the soul-quaking terror felt by Old Man Warner.

In her most overtly political novel, *The Sundial*, Jackson wonders about this human need for reactionary monstrosities, and how this compulsion to exclude Others works to shield her characters – and, vicariously, her readers – from the unconscious dread of a fully actualised democracy. After an eccentric aunt delivers to her family an apocalyptic message, the Halloran family holes up in their mansion to await the end times. The remainder of the text exposes the sociopolitical dimensions of an agoraphobic group that defines itself as 'chosen' while maintaining the pretence of democratic respectability, especially in their relationship to the local village. The leader of this group, Mrs. Halloran, fashions her deceased father as 'a democratic man' and presents his *noblesse oblige* as a sign of the family's magnanimous democratic character (Jackson 2014: 85). The Hallorans summon villagers to one last party at their manor, an event that will be followed by a closing of the gates and, or so the prophecy says, an evisceration of the populace. On the one hand, if the villagers knew their coming fate, members of Jackson's *beau monde* presume that they 'would stand with their jaws hanging, looking at each other and grinning in a foolish fashion' (200). In these moments, readers share in Mrs. Halloran's superior position as they perceive an undeserving *demos* that cannot process the horrors that have befallen it. On the other hand, by pivoting away from Mrs. Halloran's perspective, Jackson's novel highlights the craven selfishness of the Hallorans and satirises their unearned sense of entitlement. By novel's end, neither character nor reader have sorted out what a 'democratic man' would actually look like. The Hallorans return to the conventional monsters of class conflict to repress a more democratic vision.

A sign of comfort and disquiet, the cumulative image of *The Sundial* involves a character placing upon the head of another character a pagan wreath. In ancient Greece, pagan crowns marked a distinguished mortal as part of a ritual designed to deify worthy members of the *demos*. This Athenian wreath reminds Jackson's reader of the elusive democratic promise, echoed by the crowd gathered around the perimeter of the Halloran estate. Re-tracing the shape of the Athenian wreath, doubled in the symbolic space of the arena, the local crowd repeatedly encircles Jackson's gentry in a way that imprisons the family and, at the same time, recounts the unnerving openness of an unleashed egalitarianism. Calling to mind the spherical images described in the preceding section of this Element, the crowd of *The Sundial* moves in a 'circular turn', stalking 'in great circles' (Jackson 2014: 186, 201). Horrifying as well as emancipatory, the *demos* wheels about the hapless Hallorans: 'The circle went round and round' (202).

The Sundial also conjures the Athenian philosopher Plato. The Hallorans share with the Athenian philosopher a wariness of the *demos* as well as a recognition that earthly individuals exist in private worlds of their own making. A sundial provides a point of contrast between the sun, or the Truth, and deceptive shadows. Tracking the logic of Plato's metaphor to its logical conclusion, *The Sundial* closes with the leader Mrs. Halloran refusing to expose the villagers to their ignorance. Yet what exists beyond Mrs. Halloran's delusions? Following Mrs. Halloran's death, the apocalyptic text spends its last breaths wondering what comes next. 'If we are to play at all in the future', a character muses during a game of bridge, 'We must compromise our different styles' (220). The exterior to Jackson's cavernous realm is the world of tomorrow, in which the comforting shadow-play of hierarchy might no longer be upheld – a world in which 'different styles' could be 'compromised' without reliance upon petty tyrants like Mrs. Halloran. Of course, Jackson's reader never gets to see this world to come. The open-ended conclusion to *The Sundial* provocatively gestures at a society with neither castles nor moats and so Jackson's novel encourages its reader to contemplate a community constituted by a lack of clear-cut borders or overzealous stone throwers. What could be more inspiring, or bone-chilling?

Once more, democracy is a style of government constituted by its own impossibility. Even Jean-Jacques Rousseau, that most ardent of democracy's defenders, confessed that no democracy had ever really existed. Democracy must remain open-ended because the political fiction of 'the people' can at any moment rewrite its own imagined essence; it could even cease to practise democracy. True democracy perpetually rejects the imaginary ground upon which any governing regime relies. Jackson's Gothic stories sustain the democratic ideal precisely because they uphold democracy as something that can never be said aloud.

To illustrate this subversive undercurrent, let us turn to Jackson's 'The Summer People'. The elderly Allisons opt to stay longer than usual in their summer cottage; in response, their backwards neighbours decide to eject them from their midst (or so the Allisons believe). With a simmering sense of dread, 'The Summer People' never provides Jackson's reader with an unimpeded shot of its central terror; rather, the story closes with the husband and wife clinging to one another, waiting for what they feel is (long to be?) their impending comeuppance. It is a typical Jackson tale in that Jackson's reader must share in the delusion of superiority held by a pair of American elitists. The narrative voice of 'The Summer People' floats between the consciousness of the haughty Mrs. Allison and unmoored observations in which an undetermined voice initially justifies Mrs. Allison's position at the top of the social pyramid, rejecting the notion that villagers 'deserved an explanation' for her peculiar decision-making (Jackson 2010: 597). Elsewhere, this unidentified narrative voice asks its readers to share in Mrs. Allison's perspective when it considers New England stock to be 'degenerated' (596). By coercing her audience to move lockstep with Mrs. Allison in her detachment from her provincial surroundings, Jackson encouraged her reader to understand what follows – the apparently monstrous machinations of the masses – as part and parcel of the gentry's already-existing nightmare of encroachment by the *demos*. In effect, Mrs. Allison transposes her latent class anxieties into the typical reactionary horrors of Gothic fiction by demonizing her neighbours to justify her own sense of entitlement. However, because these traditional monsters remain the creations of Mrs. Allison, readers must ask what Mrs. Allison actually fears.

Beneath her performative *noblesse oblige*, Mrs. Allison remains dimly aware of her own parasitic function within the body politic. Even as she outwardly declares that the rabble depend upon her, she vaguely, perhaps even unconsciously, recognises the unsettling fact that it is she who depends upon the *demos*. Her real terror stems not from zombified masses encroaching on the domain of the wealthy, then, but from the threat that her parasitic duo will be cut off from public goods such as gas, electricity, and the postal service. The 'indefinable assets' upon which the couple begrudgingly depends become glaringly visible as the villagers realise that they no longer need the Allisons

(594). The possibility that the *demos* will dispatch with the Allisons exists as a terrifying, and seductive, hole in the middle of Jackson's story: "'But if there's no mail –,'" and leaving an awful silence behind him, [Mr. Allison] went off' (604). Jackson's surface-level horror of a steadily encroaching *demos* with ungodly appetites veils a second, far more unnerving terror: the reality that the Allisons are actually no better than anyone else.

Since 'The Summer People' remains replete with uncanny repetitions, Jackson's reader starts to suspect that the entire edifice of liberal society, built upon a stratified order that segregates the propertied class from everyone else, represses a disturbing sameness that encompasses every member of the *demos*, including the Allisons. The villagers restate what the Allisons say; the Allisons mimic the laconic style of their neighbours. The story's repetitive rhythm underscores the unnerving fact that *social difference is only ever a performance*, and so the imagined distinctions between the Allisons and the villagers are only ever a false front. Jackson's story closes with an echo heard across a lake, in anticipation of Mark Fisher's 'eerie cry', which produces 'a feeling that the enigma might involve forms of knowledge, subjectivity, and sensation that lie beyond common experience' (Fisher 2017: 62). Jackson's echo signals the eeriness of a democracy to come.

Crucially, the final echo of 'The Summer People' returns 'unwanted' (Jackson 2010: 606). Indeed, this uncomfortable feeling of being unwanted permeates the text. Translating the anxiety that their children no longer need them into the apparently more digestible register of class struggle, the Allisons must come to terms with their own irrelevance. When the Allisons blur the line between their children and the villagers, they expose their own feelings of superiority. Yet the deeper fear expressed by 'The Summer People' is that neither their children nor their neighbours actually depend upon the Allisons. In the end, Jackson's story shifts its narrative voice away from the perspective of the Allisons and into the position of the *demos* itself. The unmoored voice at last rejects the story's earlier notion that the Allisons 'deserved to hear news'; now, in the twilight of their dominance, the voice of the public 'no longer reache[s] them' (607). The Allisons secretly long to have a purpose, to belong within the body politic that they consciously reject. At the same time, their greatest nightmare is an impending democratic rearrangement in which the fiction of their own pre-eminence will be revealed to be nothing more than the stuff of fantasy.

Even as the Allisons rehearse the grotesque theatrics of class conflict, they unconsciously hold open the possibility for a levelled society in which the assets of the commons could be widely shared and in which every person depends equally upon every other person. Jackson's implicated reader must confront the layers of her own political nightmares: the first layer of horrifying Others that haunt the Allisons (as self-defined elites) and the second layer of a terrifying democracy – a radical arrangement that could never be totally actualised but proves all the more influential because of this unrealisability. Jackson's vision of democracy can be neither fetishised in the form of a tyrant nor fetishised as the composite figure of the demanding rabble. Through the ironic distance that her fiction maintains from democracy as a sublime object, Jackson allows her stories to preserve democracy's unnerving potential.

Inexorable Demagogues

One of the primary things that separates Shirley Jackson from Stephen King is their distinctive attitudes towards democracy. Although King habitually replicates Jackson's binary between elite outsider and unruly electorate, he makes a significant modification: King's outsiders are almost always blue-collar workers, and he asks his readers to share in a trustworthy narrator's dismissal of the *demos*. There is precious little ironic distance to be found. Said another way, while Jackson implicated her readers in the delusions of the well-to-do, King asks his reader to presume that the anti-democratic position of his blue-collar hero is automatically correct. He treats the lurking *demos* – its ever-present menace – as something that is both immanent and real, something always to be believed and decidedly not the fodder of a plutocrat's corrosive imagination. According to the logic of King's Gothic tales, the demagogue is the inevitable outcome of a democracy run amuck.

Collectivism, or the 'power of the people' (the literal meaning of democracy), appears to be a malevolent force for King. It manifests in novels from *Carrie*, with its mob-like mentalities, to *Dreamcatcher*, in which otherwise decent men become unwitting bullies once they join their powers to achieve common goals. In *IT*, an invisible force leads otherwise upstanding children to shun lepers, to become mirror images of their violent enemy (the Bowers gang). The so-called power of the people consolidates into hideous forms of groupthink. His novella 'The Mist' similarly focuses on members of a *demos*, sheltered in the aptly named Federal market and struggling to come to a consensus about how to face the evil outside. The educated Mr. Norton, likely a gesture by King at Ralph Ellison's benevolent tyrant from *Invisible Man*, gets busy 'spellbinding' a crowd, while the extremist Mrs. Carmody coerces a group of zealots to do her bidding (King 1985: 65). The demagogues hold something like New England town hall meetings to manipulate public opinion, and the hapless electorate follows them to their doom. Democracy in 'The Mist' arrives as if by gravitational pull at despotism; in response, the novella's hero retreats into his private bunker. King defines democracy primarily by its fetishes or, more to the point, he renders democracy and fetishism synonymous, driven by the same ignoble means to the same macabre ends. In contrast, as we have seen, Jackson's democracy exists as an impossible entity, lingering beneath hierarchical fantasies and sustaining a vital sense of unceasing discomfort for characters and readers alike. It is not as though King cannot shift into Jackson's gear – in fact, the enduring spectre of the political, which requires a foundational open-endedness, remains a vital, if unconscious, part of what makes King's fiction so compelling in the first place.[24] Still, King parts ways with Jackson with his preference for unsavoury communitarian avatars like Randall Flagg, Pennywise, or Andre Lenoge. His vision of democracy is stalled (at best) and permanently foreclosed (at worst).

At the most obvious level, King's corpus supplies a surfeit of authoritarian mouthpieces. From Kurt Barlow in '*Salem's Lot* to Big Jim Rennie in *Under the Dome*, King has long obsessed over American demagogues. But dislike of demagogues is not automatically the same as a desire for democracy. King expresses a preference for police officers above participatory governance (*From a Buick 8*) and he champions detached individuals for their refusal to enter into the political fray (*The Dead Zone*; *Insomnia*). In this sense, King's work is hardly 'democratic' in the true sense of the word. He pairs a relentless attack on authoritarians with a marked fear of democratic decision-making, which he invariably likens to corrosive groupthink. His Gothic prose makes visible what it deems to be the spirit of democracy by endowing it with a particular vessel and using the transitive properties of fantastic fiction to equate the essence of democracy with a pervasive and unsettling supernaturalism. Early observers of American democracy like Alexis de Tocqueville treated democracy like a religious revival: 'For Tocqueville, direct democracy has an almost mystical impact on citizens, as it infuses the "spirit" of democratic forms in their souls' (Field 2022: 19). King too endows democracy with talismanic qualities – this time, however, it is a demonic possession in need of immediate exorcism (in this way, as I have argued elsewhere, King may be the neoliberal writer *par excellence*).[25]

Consider the distinctive ways that Jackson and King have depicted the crowd, that most visible emblem of democracy.[26] According to Canetti, fire parallels

---

[24] As Carl Sederholm observes, 'There is no denying that Jackson haunts King's career in ways that set her apart from other influences' (Sederholm 2021: 61).

[25] See Michael J. Blouin's *Stephen King and American Politics* (Cardiff: University of Wales Press, 2021).

[26] Another example would be King's corn imagery in his short 'Children of the Corn'. Canetti argues that corn symbolises the crowd due to its striking degree of sameness and, importantly, because 'men readily see their own equality before death in the image of the corn' (Canetti 1984: 85). In King's story, corn represents the democratic mob: a group of barbaric children spellbound

the democratic crowd because it is sudden, originates anywhere, and it seems alive, restless, contagious, incendiary, and insatiable. Of note, Jackson understood well the correlation between the symbolic function of the crowd and fire when, in *We Have Always Lived in the Castle*, an unruly crowd gathers to burn down the home of an elite family. The symbols of the crowd and fire intermingle as the protagonist notes, 'I could hear [the fire] ... the voices of the people watching' (Jackson 1991b: 151). In *Needful Things*, King similarly blurs the line between fire and crowd when the town of Castle Rock literally as well as metaphorically explodes and a helpless sheriff tries to reassert his authority over the rabble. Both Jackson and King have drawn from a familiar reservoir of symbols to convey the awe-inspiring nature of the *demos* – but the results are far from the same.[27]

Whereas Jackson's crowds rupture an aristocratic illusion of calm, and thereby threaten genuine upheavals (internal as well as external), King's crowds invariably justify the wariness of his detached policeman, or characters who share a consummate psychic position with the policeman. The animalistic masses, King's fiction suggests, demand to be tamed by whip and chair. King's *Mr. Mercedes* opens with a crowd of 'agitated' welfare recipients trampling one another; the novel ends with a stampeding crowd at a concert (King 2014: 11). Jodi Dean observes, 'Inseparable from the rise of mass democracy, the crowd looms' (Dean 2016: 7). Yet, as this Element has illustrated, responses to the looming crowd within the American Gothic dramatically differ. Representative of a contemporary brand of 'democracy' that can be monitored as well as controlled, King manages his crowds by encouraging readers to ride out their irrational storms. Nevertheless, since the proverbial crowd allows 'the people' to emerge as a political subject, that is to say, since the unpredictable gathering of a crowd is precisely what makes democracy possible in the first place, Jackson's crowds unexpectedly surface to upset the fragile equilibrium of the *haut monde*. As such, Jackson's crowds recall an essential gap through which democracy threatens to surge. King's crowds, on the other hand, present an occasion for readerly revulsion as well as a fortification of border walls: a conservative reaction, triggered by a 'crowd-molting-into-mob vibe [that] is just too strong to resist' (King 2009: 471). King's corpus suggests

---

by charismatic preaching and intent upon murdering outsiders. The cultish crowd/corn instigates horror: 'He was in the corn and it closed behind him and over him like the waves of a green sea, taking him in' (King 2011: 425).

[27] In King's novel *The Outsider*, when a crowd interjects in the legal affairs of the state, it must be rebuffed: 'The spectators had become a crowd, and now the crowd teetered on the edge of mobism' (King 2018: 182).

that Americans are too afraid an empowered people; Jackson's work posits that they are not yet afraid enough.

King and Jackson have displayed distinctive approaches to what I would call the democratic secret. Jackson once stated, 'In every book I have ever written . . . I find a wall surrounding some forbidden, lovely secret, and in this wall a gate that cannot be passed' (Jackson 2016: 373). Jackson's Gothic works reflect a need to leave democracy unsaid – to guard its secret and therefore protect its indispensable impossibility. Her self-fashioned autocrats refuse to confront an egalitarian revolution that haunts their every move. King's works, on the other hand, mostly refuse to leave secrets unexposed.[28] By uttering the democratic secret, and cementing democracy's fate in the form of the demagogue, King defuses democracy's basic potential. After all, just as to say a secret aloud is no longer to hold a secret, to give a democracy given final expression is to cease to be democratic. To tease out this distinction, I will now turn to King's *Storm of the Century*, for which he penned the screenplay. The mini-series is an obvious homage to Jackson's 'The Lottery', but with significant modifications that underscore King's distinctive political overlook.

Storm features a small New England community that faces a major winter storm as well as the accompanying visit by a devilish demagogue named Andre Linoge (Colm Feore).[29] After the storm hits, town constable Mike Anderson (Tim Daly), another one of King's consummate policemen, attempts to preserve the peace as Linoge wreaks havoc by stoking panic among the townsfolk. In the closing scenes, the supernatural Linoge organises a town hall meeting and pushes the people of Little Tall Island to 'deliberate and choose' for him a child protégé. Afraid of what Linoge will do if they do not sacrifice one of their children to meet his demands, the *demos* hands him Mike's only son. *Storm* thus presents a broad and bitter indictment of democratic governance. More specifically, the mini-series manifests the premise of democracy in the highly visible, shape-shifting form of Linoge. Subverting the utopian rhetoric of Tocqueville, who saw the spirit of American democracy as the beautiful soul of a young nation, King renders democracy as an otherworldly presence that corrupts the essence of a citizenry. The story is set in 1989, ten years prior to its broadcast, and as such it inverts a popular picture: at the supposed high-water mark of American democracy, the year in which the Cold War presumably reaches its terminus, American democracy reveals itself to be a delusion . . . or a preternatural curse.

---

[28] Dara Downey and Darryl Jones affirm this difference: Jackson upheld the sanctity of the unsaid; in King's universe, 'nothing is permitted to lurk unseen' (Downey and Jones 2005: 229).

[29] In King's estimation, *Storm* is much more than a minor work; indeed, King has deemed it his 'absolute favorite' of the televised adaptations of his works (Marsh n.p.).

Unlike Jackson, who created a disjointed sense of identification in which readers align with the American aristocracy and come to know this alignment to be claustrophobic, King anchors his audience to a solid point that unequivocally orients their experience. *Storm* opens with an ominous shot of snow-covered streets as Mike's voice-over identifies him as the moral conscience of the mini-series. His voice-over alerts the spectator that she will be sharing Mike's perspective throughout, and that his voice alone as constable, enforcer of the town's laws, can be trusted. In quintessential King fashion, Mike's voice achieves this status by rehearsing a litany of blue-collar bona fides: he 'ain't a Rhodes scholar' and he doesn't know much about philosophy. King's mini-series positions Mike as a moral compass, not an intellectual. A local boy, he follows his gut instead of his head. By the time the monstrous stand-in for democracy (Linoge) rears his ugly face, King has primed his audience to cling to Mike's *a priori* sense of right and wrong. Mike's personal strengths trump the capricious character of the citizenry at Little Tall Island.

With their sinful secrets, the residents of the island require the steady hand of a pastoral overseer. They are stirred into a frenzy by the forecast of an impending winter storm and subsequently storm Mike's butcher shop to buy up as much meat as they can. A character remarks that Mike may need to use his whip and chair to tame the ensuing crowd. The audience should take Mike's notion of top-down discipline seriously since the scene in the butcher shop, with its frenzied commotion, immediately cuts to a scene of children taunting a girl who has gotten her head stuck in a staircase. Like their parents, the children of Little Tall apparently need discipline as they devolve into an imitation of monkeys. Mike and his wife Molly (Debrah Farentino) play the literal and figurative role of parents throughout the mini-series. Unlike Jackson's Allisons, though, these children do depend upon their parental figures. The one-way dependence is never questioned or treated with a sense of irony. The language of the mini-series makes the case overt: citizens cannot be trusted to govern themselves. King's hysterical *demos* simply cannot be left to its own devices.

Meanwhile, Linoge functions as the type of charlatan that King habitually denounces. He appeals to the crowd's baser emotions through elaborate spectacles designed to instill fear. A populist placeholder, he alone delivers democracy to the island. Linoge disrupts the town's normal operations by compelling citizens to take their fate into their own hands and unruly residents respond by shouting down their Selectman as well as restraining Mike. Through the sinister machinations of Linoge, the corrosive promise of democracy 'possesses' the citizenry of Little Tall Island. In one powerful dream, Linoge leads the citizens to march like blind lemmings off a pier into the teaming sea, as a close-up of King's democratic demon dissolves into shots of the storm itself. The abject force of King's malignant democracy intrudes upon innocent societies and tears them apart from within.

King's *Storm* is a companion piece to Jackson's 'The Lottery' in that both narratives detail a New England town that sacrifices one of its own citizens to satisfy the carnal cravings of democracy run amuck. Yet Jackson offered no background to the horrible ritual of 'The Lottery' and, as I have already noted, her secretive story retains the possibility that the story's barbaric stoning exercise is actually a coping mechanism to hold at bay the perceived threat of an actual democracy. King's world is far more fixed. The New England-style town hall meeting at the climax of *Storm* would have been fresh on King's mind in the late 1990s because of its resuscitation in the national imagery during the Clinton years, in which Clinton exploited the rhetoric of the town hall meeting for his national campaigns. 'Real democracy resides deep in America's dearest dreams', Frank Bryan optimistically writes of the town hall meeting. 'It is like the springtime' (Bryan 2003: 54). King's approach to the town hall meeting strikes a significantly less optimistic note: King's town hall event, quite literally buried by the furies of winter, reveals itself to be more like a nightmare from which dreamers must frantically awaken. Linoge orchestrates the meeting – he commands everyone to attend, he sets the time for deliberation, and he provides the coloured stones that townsfolk use to simulate a drawing of lots. Linoge is democracy personified.

Readers could respond to King's mini-series by blaming the individual citizens that fall prey to Linoge's advances. It is not so much democracy that is to blame, they might insist, but imperfect citizens. Rehearsing a point previously made by Rousseau, it may be that democracy only works if townships remain populated by godlike Mike Andersons. However, there are multiple reasons to persist in viewing *Storm* as an indictment of democracy as a whole, not just its flawed practitioners. Both as instrument *and* as spirit, democracy proves to be a malediction. For one, King's mini-series makes apparent how democracy can make as well as unmake itself; the *demos* needs no external referent to legitimise its decisions. According to *Storm*, the *demos* inevitably rejects Platonic guiding lights. After the lighthouse of Little Tall Island collapses, the *demos* will be left to its own devices. King's quarrel with democracy is not what the town does under its spell, then, but how the town does it. In other words, King's problem remains the logic of democracy itself.

Audiences might interrogate how American democracy fails in *Storm*. Mike's wife Molly defends the town's decision to draw lots; she contends that the Andersons have enjoyed the luxury of being a part of the island democracy and so they are dutybound to respect its mode of making decisions, even when the decisions do not favour them. When Molly later recants her position upon the random selection of their son, Linoge reminds her, just as the villagers remind their victim at the close of Jackson's 'The Lottery', that the game was fair and that everyone took the same chance by submitting to the democratic process. As such, Molly's principled stance mirrors the position of Socrates in his well-known 'Crito': the Athenian mob may be reaching an erroneous conclusion by condemning Socrates to death but he fashions himself a law-abiding citizen and so he must not run away. When viewed in a Socratic light, Molly's position may seem entirely rational – unless one admits that *the game itself is the problem*. James Madison once reasoned: 'Had every Athenian citizen been a Socrates, every Athenian Assembly would still have been a mob' (Madison 1961: 374). In his final voice-over, Mike wishes Molly well in her next marriage, encouraging King's audience not to blame the individual participants but to fear instead the spellbinding power of democracy as a concept.

Even the sheriff Mike occasionally appeals to the panacea of democracy. You elected me to be your constable, he tells the people, so let me do my job. Yet Mike's *a priori* morality, the guiding light that stands tall among little citizens below, defies the democratic premise because the 'right thing to do' is always-already spelled out and requires no input from a fickle electorate. Manifested in the laurels that it bestows upon Mike, King's mini-series celebrates the inter-ventions of a philosopher-king or, more accurately, a blue-collar king. King stands out as a pre-eminent purveyor of epistocracy (a governing mode that cedes power to the most knowledgeable citizens). King's hair-raising demo-cratic storm caters to the whims of a tyrannical majority, disguises brutal self-interest as collective reasoning, and abolishes eternal truths in favour of decisions that practitioners rashly revise upon a moment's notice. Better to hand the reins to a Platonic protagonist like Mike, King decrees.

King's critique of democracy has several inconsistencies. For instance, after the atrocities of the town hall meeting, Mike's former friend apologises for making the wrong decision. Mike grimly reminds him that what's done is done. In other words, the horror of King's democracy is that even though it can undo its own former proclamations, like stripping Mike of his authority as constable or violating the basic rights of its youngest citizens, the democracy of Little Tall Island apparently cannot reverse itself when it comes to its more disagreeable business. Specifically, in the case of forfeiting Mike's child, what is done must remain done. For King, then, democracy remains entirely too permeable by design. It lacks a Platonic lighthouse, and at the same time it remains entirely too rigid, given the apparent irreversibility of its less desirous decisions. King's democracy is stuck in a damaging cyclical pattern that can be forecast but never avoided.

Embodied in the visceral form of Linoge, King's democracy remains always-already wicked. As we saw in the previous section, Jackson's Gothic vision of democracy remains a dynamic one thanks to 'the permanent renewal of [democracy's] enigma' (Plot 2014: 19). In contrast, King's texts do not leave open the heart of democracy, or tarry with its constitutional impossibility. King's democracy plagues American audiences as a fetishised monster rather than an unrealisable spectre. Marcel Gauchet insists that 'a democratic consciousness worthy of the name' must acknowledge that democracy's 'realization [remains] impossible' (Gauchet 2022: 191). As such, Jackson's fiction effectively holds open the opportunity for a democratic future. But a crucial question remains: can the American Gothic ever represent an embodied democratic experience – a living, breathing phenomenon – without relying upon King's reactionary monsters? That is, could the immaterial dynamism of Jackson's democracy ever be integrated successfully into a *tangible* form? Which will it be: the fetish or the abyss? Bearing down upon our little islands, the spectre of democracy (horrifically; mercifully) endures.

5 The Requisite Fears of Democracy

To varying degrees, the horror films written and directed by Jordan Peele highlight the hypocrisies of American democracy. They feature alienated Black characters that grapple with their oppression within a system that proclaims itself to be equitable. For example, Peele's first film *Get Out* tracks a young Black man as an ostensibly welcoming white family reveals that it has nefarious plans to exploit him. This chapter will turn to Peele's 2019 release *Us* to show how American democracy remains in no small part driven by reactionary horrors. And yet the film also holds that a healthy democracy must maintain a sense of terror: a terror that precariously holds 'us' together through traumatic ruptures, inevitable gaps, and the simmering dread of what cannot be known.[30] According to *Us*, the horror film is a vital instrument for re-theorising what has become, in popular discourse at least, a rather bullish democratic utopianism.

Peele's title foregrounds a dialectic: the title remains both particular (the film focuses upon the United States) and universal ('Us' could mean everyone within earshot). In turn, the film asks penetrating questions about the nature of the nation's democratic promise. Must democracy be premised upon a veiled exclusion, what political philosopher Carl Schmitt calls the friend/enemy

---

[30] According to Judith Butler, the United States needs democratic reforms to encourage citizens to abandon abstract (and dangerous) belief in a sense of fullness, of total belonging, and to feel in its place a deeper attachment to what Butler calls the injurious name: a traumatic lack that characterises a more ethical form of citizenship.

distinction, and, if so, why should disenfranchised subjects continue to believe in greater enfranchisement as their sole salvation? Is democracy doomed to warfare between parties defined by their prescriptive racial, ethnic, and cultural identities, or should it be rooted in an all-embracing Us? In its attempt to address these questions, Peele's *Us* highlights a constitutive tension between the *horrors* of democracy – the need for monstrous Others to rally a cohesive unit, for example, the countless bourgeois family clans that endure at the close of Hollywood horror films – and the *terrors* of democracy – specifically, the prospect of a totalised equality, or a democratic sublime. By tarrying at this fault line, *Us* reveals the horror film to be a vehicle for re-imagining the perils as well as the possibilities of America's beleaguered democratic project.

While on vacation in Santa Cruz, the Wilson family uncovers the troubled past of the maternal Adelaide (Lupita Nyong'o). When she was a child, Adelaide ventured into a tunnel beneath the Santa Cruz boardwalk labelled 'Vision Quest: Find Yourself'. Once inside the dark underbelly, Adelaide's double accosted her, took her place, and left the young girl handcuffed to a bunkbed in a strange underground lair. The audience learns that the government has been experimenting with doubles, soulless zombies known as the tethered which were designed to mimic their *doppelgängers* above the surface. When the 'real' Adelaide arrives, the subterranean populace begins to plot an insurrection against its above-ground counterpart. Flash forward to the present: the Wilsons must face off against their doubles, dispatching them in grisly fashion. At film's end, as the tethered coalition forms a line of protesters across the nation, Adelaide remembers that she herself started underground, which is to say, she is actually the tethered version of herself. Because *Us* renders egalitarian connectivity as a grotesque proposition, at times ironically and at times with apparent sincerity, Peele's audience cannot too quickly romanticise the consensual Oneness pictured at the close of the film – the solidarity of an unfathomable line of individuals, joined together to evoke seismic change. *Us* challenges the democratic fantasies of countless American spectators by exposing their reactionary horrors as well as their revolutionary terrors.

A democratic contradiction drives Peele's film. On the one hand, *Us* channels a widespread fear of egalitarianism as the Wilson family rallies against the collectivist revolution at hand. The film upholds in these moments a rampant bourgeois tribalisation. Many Americans remain entirely too afraid of democracy, especially when it threatens a relatively stable economic situation for the individual in question. On the other hand, *Us* rejects the pre-supposition that 'the [horror] genre cannot formulate that the problem is a collective one rather than one that besets a small familial group' (McGowan 2019: 66). Peele's film claims that a sublime unity exists not in what binds reactionary groups together but in what each group as well as each of its members cannot secure. A mother kills the thing that ostensibly made her whole; a son chooses to wear a mask to protect himself from the knowing gaze of a parent. The film features countless traumatic remainders of what has been excluded from the imagined general will. Peele's alternative vision of togetherness preserves a vital sense of estrangement and it thus underscores how absence, instead of utopian consensus, defines a democratic polis. When it comes to their feelings about democracy, *Us* posits, many Americans have not yet reckoned with the *necessity* of a fear that makes the system work.

But let us unpack first the reactionary horrors critiqued throughout the film. Like most of the Gothic figures considered in the preceding sections, Peele's spectator shares in the angst of the privileged caste as they face an encroaching horde of dispossessed beings. In these moments, *Us* assumes the singular perspective of a subject that has benefited from the unfair advantages of what has been labelled as white democracy: a society designed to benefit the white majority under the guise of universal inclusivity. However unconsciously, the Wilsons identify with a white majority. The parents encourage their daughter to 'shoot for the stars' and reassure her that she can achieve whatever she sets out to achieve. As Peele's film unreservedly demonstrates, these platitudes ought to sound nonsensical to people of colour living in America. *Us* exposes the myth of equality, the defining trait of an assumed democracy, to be a fiction as Peele's characters as well as his audience realise that the game has been rigged. With its faux fraternity as well as its phony sense of patriotic unity, the rhetoric of the Hands Across America campaign, which appears frequently in the film, represses the inconvenient truth that the fable of equal opportunity in the United States has evolved in parallel with brutal acts of exclusion of women, indigenous peoples, and enslaved individuals (the list goes on). Adelaide's son Jason (Evan Alex) glimpses this macabre reality when he walks in on his mother bludgeoning one of the tethered. As they relish in violence against the tethered, Peele's characters appear to be enjoying democracy precisely because of its tendency towards tribalisation. Unlike the platitudes of egalitarian love that countless Americans consume on a daily basis, Peele's *Us* contends that democracy in the United States has long been driven by the perverse pleasures associated with a graphic destruction of Others. Reactionary horrors propel American democracy.

Cornel West would likely agree with Peele's opening salvo: 'Race is the crucial intersection point where democratic energies clash with American imperial realities' (West 2005: 14). Nevertheless, although he remains wary of forces that appropriate the idea of democracy for exploitative ends, West sustains 'a deep public reverence for – a love of – democracy in America' (15).

Peele's *Us* will not let its audience off the hook so easily. Instead, it claims that democracy is neither a symptom of a latent loving culture nor an expression of America's intrinsic conciliatory tendencies. No, democratic energies do not 'clash with' American imperialism; they sustain it. 'Racial oppression and American democracy are mutually constitutive' (Olson 2004: xv). At their most fundamental level, the concept of race and democracy necessitate the consolidation of individuals under joint identity markers, and they generate forms of solidarity through an active exclusion of imagined outsiders. A problem therefore arises within the very logic of American democracy, as the loosely defined tribal bloc of 'whiteness' presents an unfair advantage. Historically, white democracy has erected an insurmountable barrier to entry for certain citizens (or non-citizens, as the case may be). It has promised equal opportunity but aggressively restricted the participation of subjects deemed to be non-white. When the tethered arrives, members of the Wilson clan awaken from their slumber and realise that their attempt to 'keep up with the Joneses' – their obnoxious white friends who own a mansion and a fleet of expensive vehicles – has been a fool's errand. Their sense of friendly competition has in truth been founded upon violent, exclusionary principles. The family's white friend (Tim Heidecker) looks out his window and jokes that he has identified an impending intruder as O.J. Simpson, a well-known football star accused of murdering his wife. Regardless of the specific details of the case itself, the Simpson trial was a public spectacle that unified predominantly white spectators in their sense of civic justice by rallying them against a single Black man.

Christina Beltran recycles the term *Herrenvolk* democracy, or a democracy designed exclusively for a 'master race' (Beltran 2020: 14). Beltran demonstrates how 'democratic feeling' became pervasive in the United States alongside, and not in distinction from, narratives of white supremacy. She holds that the gloss of a participatory ethos in American democracy has been secured through laws that embolden white supremacists and reduce the participation of subjects that it deems to be non-white. 'Civic creation', Beltran points out, has long involved 'acts of racialised violence'. That is to say, democratic citizenship has been upheld in the United States by 'deprivation, exclusion, suffering, and removal . . . a recursive scarcity logic that premises one's own thriving in the denial of such thriving of others' (42, 30–31). *Us* similarly exposes the sanguineous machinations of a *Herrenvolk* democracy by solidifying a normative family unit (the Wilsons) that expels the tethered from its ancestral cabin. Through their aggressive expulsion of the Other, the Wilsons re-enact the barbarism of belonging that accompanies any *Herrenvolk* democracy. The clichéd stick family decal on the back of the Wilson vehicle foreshadows the eventual restoration of a bourgeois clan that must either fall in line with the basic precepts of white democracy or 'get out'. The preceding sections uncover how this sort of reactionary consolidation occurs in the American Gothic, from works by Washington Irving to the tales of H.P Lovecraft. The horror of a democratic mob storming the proverbial castle evokes a strong urge to rally the privileged few into a posture of self-defence. American horror stories incessantly fantasise about a democratic society upheld by an exclusion of the Other.

On a related note, as a tale about doubles, Peele's film reflects upon a general anxiety felt by Americans regarding the concept of an unchecked egalitarianism. Parodying the anti-democratic spirit of Edgar Allan Poe, the name of Peele's family echoes Poe's short story 'William Wilson', discussed at length in the second section of this Element. Once relatively comfortable in their alignment with white democracy, members of the Wilson family are confronted by their own unexceptional status when their duplicates arrive on the scene. Like the self-defined elites of Shirley Jackson's fiction, the Wilsons initially try to re-contain the tethered versions of themselves by transposing their doubles into a monstrous register, a tactic quickly swatted away by Adelaide's double Red. 'What are you people?' one of the Wilsons inquires, dehumanising his double by treating him as a 'what' instead of a 'who'. Red confidently replies: 'We're Americans'. Red later indignantly reminds her privileged counterpart, 'We're human, too, you know'. Despite efforts by the Wilsons to treat their doubles as abject Others, *Us* reminds its audience of the uncomfortable fact that these doubles are worthy of equal standing. After all, the maternal protagonist is herself one of the tethered. The fear that Peele's film conveys is distinctive from Poe's trepidation, however, because rather than position the anxiety of a displaced privileged caste at the fore of the film, it foregrounds the anxiety of disenfranchised people of colour: ostracised individuals forced to confront the grim reality that they will never be included within the victorious majority due to the colour of their skin.[31] Without the imagined refuge of an exclusionary whiteness, the Wilsons must inevitably join their doubles not as equal citizens but as invisible beings, segregated, like Ralph Ellison's eponymous character, in the sewers. The promise of democratic equality only ever sooths citizens that already enjoy the privilege of aligning with an established majority as a result of the phenotype with which they were born. To cite Juliet Hooker, Peele's horrifying portrayal of democratic consensus, infused with Adelaide's as well as Red's painful sense of Black grief, differs in kind from Poe's horrifying

---

[31] As James Baldwin notes, 'In a group so pressed down, terrified and at bay and carrying generations of constricted, subterranean hostility, no real group identification is possible' (Baldwin 1998: 581).

portrayal of egalitarianism, infused as it is with Poe's white grievances as a self-fashioned Southern elite.

Despite their status as outsiders, Adelaide as well as Red ignore their shared grief and persist in a kind of democratic utopianism. Adelaide suppresses the egalitarian fright caused by her double by reasserting, 'Everything's going to be like it was before'; meanwhile, Red recycles theological language to envision a joint soul or, as she puts it, 'One shared by Two'. Red speaks prophetically when she tells Adelaide, 'God brought us together that night', and she judges her counterpart's ethics when she states, 'You could have taken me with you'. This viewpoint explains why the tethered do not technically free themselves at the end of the film; instead, they join hands to become tethered once more. This reactionary unification conveys the excessive fear of a typical American when confronted by the radical differences of a genuine democracy. Said another way, the tethered, with their limited vision of democracy, ultimately erase all signs of difference to (re)achieve an illusion of unity. *But democracy is antagonistic or it is nothing at all* – a reality that remains its truest terror. Democracy demands difference, or the open-endedness of a society occupied by citizens with variegated desires.

The closing shot of *Us* gestures at an uncertainty that cannot be resolved. The final image is a perfect example of the democratic sublime: members of the tethered spread out across the land and, borrowing the language of the Hands Across America movement, stretch 'from sea to shining sea'. Peele's spectator gazes down upon the masses, linked together to achieve collective ends. The father of the Wilson clan describes the crowd as 'a group engaged in demonstration, or protest' – a movement that took 'a shitload of coordination'. This democratic movement cannot be confined to a television screen or a cheesy t-shirt logo; it explodes beyond the margins of the screen itself. The son Jason asks, 'How many of everybody is there going to be?' According to the film's form as well as its content, the answer to Jason's question remains unfathomable.

Us repeatedly gestures at the democratic multitude, or the empowered 'people'. When members of the tethered first arrive, the young Adelaide stands at the edge of the sea, drawing Peele's spectators into marvelling at the sights and sounds of the vast ocean. Once inside of the haunted hall of mirrors, spectators glimpse a refracted EXIT sign. At the exact moment that a revolution ruptures the status quo, Peele's film conjures the theoretical work of Michael Hardt and Antonio Negri by making it possible for audiences to imagine a limitless number of pathways out of the current social arrangement. In each of these instances, the democratic revolution creates a gap, both within the diegetic world and in the manner with which audiences visualise that revolution. According to Peele's film, democracy is like a boundless sea or a hall of mirrors. It endures not because of a latent will to wholeness, then, but because of the holes that puncture the subject's comprehension of a fully realised democratic ideal. Joan Copjec describes something like the democratic sublime when she writes, 'Democracy is not a utopia ... Democracy seems designed [. . .] to acknowledge the impossibility of its alleviation ... it is only because I doubt that I am therefore a democratic citizen' (Copjec 1994: 161).[32] Dystopian, impossible, shrouded in doubt: it is not as though the American Gothic monopolises these emotions, of course, but it does dramatically heighten them. Adapting Poe's aggrieved imagination to the grief of being Black in America, Peele's film tarries around a figurative pit: a conceptual chasm that evades the mind's capacity to understand it, not unlike the perilous well at the centre of *Get Out*. Ontologically speaking, democratic subjects like Adelaide/ Red must reopen the traumatic rupture between their reactionary identity markers (cohesive; coherent) and the thrilling as well as terrifying reality that, within their democratic arrangement, they must make themselves endlessly anew. As a result, these encounters with the democratic sublime might stop American democracy from settling into a deficient or dead-end version of itself.

Despite the fact that Peele's film relentlessly references the tribal logic that undergirds Hollywood horror, from Stephen Spielberg's *Jaws* to Stanley Kubrick's *The Shining*, this tribal logic cannot endure in the face of the film's repetition with difference. As the Wilsons drive over the horizon into the unknown in the dwindling moments of the story, something fundamental within the film's formulaic structure has changed. What appears to be the tight-knit unity of the Wilson clan – forged in the fires of an obscene amount of violence – bears a striking resemblance to the outcome of myriad horror films. However, the film's return to unity within a small unit is not quite the same as the regressive conclusions of the works being referenced. What glues the Wilsons together is not a compulsory destruction of monstrous Others, or a naïve return to romanticised Oneness, but a knowledge that every member of the family persists as a traumatised, incomplete being. They have viscerally killed off their shadows and in so doing revealed themselves to be utterly lacking: the One become Two. Any hope for a utopian resolution or reconciliation reveals itself to be a lost cause. For the Wilsons, the brutal enjoyment of tribal democracy (its unsavoury, inegalitarian horrors) has been replaced by a sense of belonging that doubles as a sense of estrangement, of non-belonging – its core egalitarian terror. Consider Adelaide's enigmatic look as Jason pulls his mask back down over his face at the close of the film, or the moment in which Jason and his

---

[32] Todd McGowan observes, 'The point of political struggle is not to include all within the social structure but to recognise the failure of all inclusion ... [a] solidarity organised around a shared absence' (McGowan 2020: 186).

double sit in the closet and reach a tentative understanding because of their shared status as masked outsiders (**Figure 7**).

The Wilson tribe has been irrevocably ruptured by the realisation that its members must remain alienated from each other as well as from themselves. The defiant solidarity that congeals in the closing moments of *Us* is haunted, then, by what has been erased over the course of the film. To illustrate this point, the film lingers upon Red as she severs the link between herself and Adelaide, in a shot that juxtaposes her severing of the bond with an interminable series of linked figures that Red has drawn on the blackboard behind her (**Figure 8**).

Peele's alternative democratic vision is precariously, and fearfully, created from the broken bonds of particular subjects, joined in their singularities to face an unknowable future. The final 'Us' of the Wilson clan suggests that the (impossible) promise of democratic solidarity should be based in trauma and terror rather than wholeness and horror.

Peele's American democracy proves to be a dark romance. In part because of its structural logic as a horror film, *Us* remains dissatisfied with utopian resolutions and unconvinced by calls for ever more participation, more voting, more democracy. The film in turn asks what could possibly come next for America's dysfunctional democracy. Which is more unsettling, a never-ending antagonism between groups or a blanket egalitarianism that erases differences? Particularly when one considers the perspective of disenfranchised people of colour, the dread of democracy reveals itself to be a complex conundrum. The kind of democracy that *Us* endorses is a distinctly Gothic one.

Figure 7 Jason (Evan Alex) identifies with his double Pluto
as masked outsiders

Credit: Blumhouse Productions / Universal Pictures / Monkeypaw Produ / Album / Alamy Stock Photo

Figure 8 This shot juxtaposes the severed bond between two stick figures with the interminable collective that sprawls across the blackboard

Credit: Blumhouse Productions / Universal Pictures / Monkeypaw Produ / Album / Alamy Stock Photo

Far removed from idyllic eulogies to democratic decline, *Us* underscores how the American Gothic can contribute to ongoing fights to revamp the nation's democratic project.[33] As Peele's horror film illustrates, the Gothic imaginary lends itself well to the ceaseless imperfection required of a functional democracy.[34] Consider the helicopter shot of the boundless tethered: the sheer vastness of the democratic sublime compels character and spectator alike into reactionary groupings; concurrently, though, this sublime shot disrupts the conventional hierarchies that have historically constituted Hollywood horror. In dialectical fashion, the dizzying spell cast by the prospect of an unfettered, all-encompassing *demos* is then broken by the last-second encroachment of military helicopters, presumably sent to re-establish a white democracy with

---

[33] Chantal Mouffe has spent her career unpacking this paradox. A democracy can only sustain its political nature when it maintains its exclusionary thrust. Democracy must remain 'contingent and open to contestation. What characterises democratic politics is the confrontation between conflicting hegemonic projects, a confrontation with no possibility of final reconciliation' (Mouffe 2013: 17). Yet Mouffe distinguishes her vision of democracy from the violent visions of Carl Schmitt by attempting to sustain belief in a universal thread, which is to say, in a universal state of particularity, or a state of incompleteness that actually binds every individual together and makes democracy a joint project.

[34] Etienne Balibar uses the term exclusive democracy: on the one side, the horrors of white democracy, its 'processes of exclusion', integrate a 'community of citizens'; on the other side, these terrifying 'limits' compel citizens to go beyond their exclusionary mindsets in the name of achieving 'universalistic ideals' (Balibar 2014: 207).

extreme prejudice. This fleeting glimpse of a Gothicised democracy – or democratised Gothic – leaves Peele's audience appropriately unsettled. *Us* reveals that although democracy depends upon pleasures tied to the inegalitarian horror of demonised Others storming the gates (a particular Us), it also retains the pleasurable power of an egalitarian movement that can terrify the establishment through moments of soul-quaking alarm (a universal Us).

The soul-quaking alarm triggered by the closing moments of *Us* is the terror of a democracy that has never really asked its white citizens to fear losing their hold on power.[35] Because all citizens are not called on to make themselves equally vulnerable in a white democracy, the experience of democracy for most white citizens has been relatively stable, comfortable, and, one might say, undemocratic. Therefore, the imagined transfer of political loss in *Us*, from Adelaide/Red to the spectator, serves as a meaningful corrective for a curated democracy that has not yet lived up to its own terrifying premise, in part because it has dwelt upon white grievance rather than Black grief. And American democracy might be better equipped to survive if spectators could confront, through Gothic encounters, the unexpected enjoyment that accompanies the terrors of a democratic experiment. Peele's spectators ought to emerge from the darkened theatre having realised that they are too fearful of democracy and, at the same time, not yet fearful enough. Like the stalwart spectator that looks to the horror film for both pain and pleasure, Peele's audience finds unexpected insights as well as delights in democracy's most Gothic elements.

---

[35] Juliet Hooker demonstrates that white democracy depends upon an uneven distribution of loss: 'Political loss is widespread in democracy but is considered legitimate insofar as it is equally distributed. Historically, however, US democracy has never distributed loss equitably' (Hooker 2023: 10).

References

J. Adams, 'Discourses on Davila', in John Patrick Diggins (ed.), *The Portable John Adams* (New York: Penguin, 2004), pp. 337–395.

D. Allen, *Talking to Strangers: Anxieties of Citizenship Since Brown v. Board of Education* (Chicago, IL: University of Chicago Press, 2004).

J. Baldwin, 'History as Nightmare', in Toni Morrison (ed.), *James Baldwin: Collected Essays* (New York: Library of America, 1998), pp. 579–582.

E. Balibar, *Equaliberty: Political Essays*, trans. James Ingram (Durham, NC: Duke University Press, 2014).

P. Barnard and S. Shapiro, 'Un-Noveling Brown: Liberalism and Its Literary Discontents', *Early American Literature*, vol. 57, no. 2 (2022), 549–554.

C. Beltran, *Cruelty as Citizenship: How Migrant Suffering Sustains White Democracy* (Minneapolis, MN: University of Minnesota Press, 2020).

D. Berthold, 'Democracy and Its Discontents', in Wyn Kelley (ed.), *A Companion to Herman Melville* (London: Blackwell, 2006), pp. 149–164.

H. Bloom, 'Introduction', in Harold Bloom (ed.), *Modern Critical Views: Edgar Allan Poe* (New York: Chelsea House, 1985), pp. 1–14.

T. Britt, 'Common Property of the Mob: Democracy and Identity in Poe's "William Wilson"'. *The Mississippi Quarterly*, vol. 47, no. 2 (Spring 1995), 197–210.

C.B. Brown, *Edgar Huntly* (New Haven, CT: New College and University Press, 1973).

F. Bryan, *Real Democracy: New England Town Meeting and How It Works*, 2nd ed., (Chicago, IL: University of Chicago Press, 2003).

A. Burstein, *Sentimental Democracy: The Evolution of America's Romantic Self-Image* (New York: Hill and Wang, 2000).

J. Butler, *The Psychic Life of Power: Theories of Subjection* (Stanford, CA: Stanford University Press, 1997).

H. Canby, *Classic Americans: A Study of Eminent American Writers from Irving to Whitman* (New York: Harcourt, Brace, 1931).

E. Canetti, *Crowds and Power*, trans. Carol Stewart (New York: Farrar, Straus and Giroux, 1984).

J. Copjec, *Read My Desire: Lacan against the Historicists* (Cambridge, MA: MIT Press, 1994).

S. Cotlar, *Tom Paine's America: The Rise and Fall of Transatlantic Radicalism in the Early Republic* (Charlottesville, VA: University of Virginia Press, 2014).

B. Crick, *Democracy: A Very Short Introduction* (Oxford: Oxford University Press, 2003).

J. Dean, *Crowds and Party* (London: Verso, 2016).

J. Derrida, *Rogues: Two Essays on Reason*, trans. Pascale-Anne Brault and Michael Naas (Stanford, CA: Stanford University Press, 2005).

W. Dillingham, *Melville's Short Fiction, 1853–1856* (Athens, GA: University of Georgia, 2008).

P. Downes, 'Democratic Terror in "My Kinsman Major Molineux" and "The Man of the Crowd"', *Poe Studies/Dark Romanticism*, vol. 27 (2004), 31–35.

D. Downey and D. Jones, 'King of the Castle: Shirley Jackson and Stephen King', in Bernice M. Murphy (ed.), *Shirley Jackson: Essays on the Literary Legacy* (Jefferson, NC: McFarland, 2005), pp. 214–236.

R. DuFord, *Solidarity in Conflict: A Democratic Theory* (Stanford, CA: Stanford University Press, 2022).

M. M. Elbert, '"The Man of the Crowd" and the Man Outside the Crowd: Poe's Narrator and the Democratic Reader', *Modern Language Studies*, vol. 21, no. 4 (1991), 16–30.

D.B. Emerson, 'George Lippard's *The Quaker City*: Disjointed Text, Dismembered Bodies, Regenerated Democracy', *Nineteenth-Century Literature*, vol. 70, no. 1 (2015), 102–131.

R.W. Emerson, 'Circles', in Joel Porte (ed.), *Emerson: Essays and Lectures* (New York: Library of America, 1983a), pp. 401–415.

R.W. Emerson, 'The Conduct of Life', in Joel Porte (ed.), *Emerson: Essays and Lectures* (New York: Library of America, 1983b), pp. 937–1125.

R.W. Emerson, 'The American Scholar', in Brooks Atkinson (ed.), *The Essential Writings of Ralph Waldo Emerson* (New York: Modern Library, 2000), pp. 43–63.

D. Faherty, '"A Certain Unity of Design": Edgar Allan Poe's "Tales of the Grotesque and Arabesque" and the Terrors of Jacksonian Democracy', *Edgar Allan Poe Review*, vol. 6, no. 2 (Fall 2005), 4–21.

D. Feller, *The Jacksonian Promise: America, 1815–1840* (Baltimore, MD: Johns Hopkins University Press, 1995).

J. Field, *Town Hall Meetings and the Death of Deliberation: Revised Edition* (Minneapolis, MN: University of Minnesota Press, 2022).

M. Fisher, *The Weird and the Eerie* (London: Repeater, 2017).

R. Formisano, *For the People: American Populist Movements* (Chapel Hill, NC: University of North Carolina Press, 2008).

F. Furet, *Revolutionary France: 1770–1880*, trans. Antonio Nevill (New York: Wiley-Blackwell, 1995).

A. Galluzzo, '*Wieland* and the Aesthetics of Terror: Revolution, Reaction, and the Radical Enlightenment in Early American Letters', *Eighteenth-Century Studies*, vol. 42, no. 2 (2009), 255–271.

M. Gauchet, 'Tocqueville, America, and Us: On the Genesis of Democratic Societies', *The Tocqueville Review*, vol. 37, no. 2 (2016), 172–224.

M. Gauchet, *Robespierre: The Man Who Divides Us Most*, trans. Malcolm DeBevoise (Princeton, NJ: Princeton University Press, 2022).

W. Godwin, *An Enquiry Concerning Political Justice* (Oxford: Oxford University Press, 2013).

M.O. Grenby, *The Anti-Jacobin Novel: British Conservatism and the French Revolution* (Cambridge: Cambridge University Press, 2005).

M. Hardt, *Michael Hardt Presents Thomas Jefferson: The Declaration of Independence* (London: Verso, 2019).

N. Hawthorne, 'Alice Doane's Appeal', in Rose Hawthorne Lathrop (ed.), *The Complete Tales of Nathaniel Hawthorne* (Boston, MA: Houghton Mifflin, 1883), pp. 279–299.

N. Hawthorne, 'My Kinsman, Major Molineux', in James McIntosh (ed.), *Nathaniel Hawthorne's Tales* (New York: W.W. Norton, 1987a), pp. 3–17.

N. Hawthorne, 'Young Goodman Brown', in James McIntosh (ed.), *Nathaniel Hawthorne's Tales* (New York: W.W. Norton, 1987b), pp. 65–75.

N. Hawthorne, *The Selected Letters of Nathaniel Hawthorne*, Joel Myerson (ed.), (Columbus, OH: Ohio State University Press, 2002).

N. Hawthorne, *The House of the Seven Gables* (New York: W.W. Norton, 2005).

J. Hogle, 'Introduction: The Gothic in Western Culture', in Jerrold Hogle (ed.), *The Cambridge Companion to Gothic Fiction* (Cambridge: Cambridge University Press, 2002), pp. 1–21.

B. Honig, *Democracy and the Foreigner* (Princeton, NJ: Princeton University Press, 2001).

J. Hooker, *Black Grief, White Grievance: The Politics of Loss* (Princeton, NJ: Princeton University Press, 2023).

W. Irving, 'The Adventure of the German Student', in Charles Neiders (ed.), *The Complete Tales of Washington Irving* (New York: De Capo Press, 1998), pp. 223–228.

H. Jackson, *American Radicals: How Nineteenth-Century Protest Shaped the Nation* (New York: Crown, 2019).

S. Jackson, 'The Lottery', in *The Lottery and Other Stories* (New York: Quality Paperback Book Club, 1991a), pp. 291–306.

S. Jackson, *We Have Always Lived in the Castle*, in *The Lottery and Other Stories* (New York: Quality Paperback Book Club, 1991b), pp. 1–214.

S. Jackson, 'The Summer People', in Joyce Carol Oates (ed.), *Shirley Jackson: Novels and Stories* (New York: Library of America, 2010), pp. 594–607.

S. Jackson, *The Sundial: Reprint Edition* (New York: Penguin Classics, 2014).

S. Jackson, 'About the End of the World', in Laurence Hyman (ed.), *Let Me Tell You: New Stories, Essays, and Other Writings* (New York: Random House, 2016), pp. 373–375.

S. Jackson, *The Letters of Shirley Jackson*, Bernice M. Murphy (ed.), (New York: Random House, 2022).

S.T. Joshi, *H.P. Lovecraft: A Life* (Warwick, RI: Necronomicon Press, 1996).

P. Kafer, *Charles Brockden Brown's Revolution and the Birth of the American Gothic* (Philadelphia, PA: University of Pennsylvania Press, 2004).

S. King, 'The Mist', in *Skeleton Crew* (New York: Signet, 1985), pp. 24–155.

S. King, *IT* (New York: Signet, 1986).

S. King, *The Stand: Unabridged Edition* (New York: Signet, 1991).

S. King, *Under the Dome* (New York: Scribner, 2009).

S. King, 'Children of the Corn', in *Night Shift* (New York: Anchor, 2011), pp. 390–434.

S. King, *Mr. Mercedes* (New York: Gallery Books, 2014).

S. King, *The Outsider* (New York: Scribner, 2018).

K. Larson, *Imagining Inequality in Nineteenth-Century American Literature* (Cambridge: Cambridge University Press, 2008).

C. Lefort, *Democracy and Political Theory*, trans. David Macey (Minneapolis, MN: University of Minnesota Press, 1988).

V. Lenin, *State and Revolution* (Leftist Public Domain Project, 2019).

P. Linebaugh and M. Rediker, *The Many-Headed Hydra: Sailors, Slaves, Commoners, and the Hidden History of the Revolutionary Atlantic*, 2nd ed., (Boston, MA: Beacon Press, 2013).

G. Lippard, 'Thomas Paine: Author-Soldier of the American Revolution — Reprinted' (Philadelphia, PA: City Institute, 1894).

G. Lippard, *The Quaker City; or, the Monks of Monk Hall* (Amherst, MA: University of Massachusetts Press, 1995).

A. Lloyd-Smith, *American Gothic Fiction: An Introduction* (New York: Continuum, 2004).

H.P. Lovecraft, 'The Horror at Red Hook', in Peter Straub (ed.), *H.P. Lovecraft: Tales* (New York: Library of America, 2005a), pp. 125–147.

H.P. Lovecraft, *Letters to Reinhart Kleine*, S. T. Joshi and David Schultz (eds.) (New York: Hippocampus Press, 2005b).

H.P. Lovecraft, 'The Rats in the Walls', in Peter Straub (ed.), *H.P. Lovecraft: Tales* (New York: Library of America, 2005c), pp. 77–97.

H.P. Lovecraft, 'The Festival', in Eric Link (ed.), *The Complete Tales of H.P. Lovecraft* (New York: Quarto, 2019a), pp. 281–288.

H.P. Lovecraft, 'The Street', in Eric Link (ed.), *The Complete Tales of H.P. Lovecraft* (New York: Quarto, 2019b), pp. 70–75.

H.P. Lovecraft, *Supernatural Horror in Literature* (Bristol: Read, 2020).

P. MacCormack, 'Lovecraft's Cosmic Ethics', in Jeffrey Weinstock and Carl Sederholm (eds.), *The Age of Lovecraft* (Minneapolis, MN: University of Minnesota Press, 2016), pp. 199–215.

J. Madison, *Federalist Papers* (Middletown, CT: Wesleyan University Press, 1961).

D. Malachuk, 'Romanticism and Democracy', in Phillip Loffler, Clemens Spahr, and Jan Stievermann (eds.), *Handbook of American Romanticism* (Boston, MA: De Gruyter, 2021), pp. 143–161.

C. Marsh, 'Stephen King Has Thoughts about Stephen King TV Shows', *The New York Times*, 14 December 2020, www.nytimes.com/2020/12/14/arts/television/stephen-king-adaptations-the-stand.html. Accessed 2 October 2022.

R. Martin, *Hero, Captain, and Stranger: Male Friendship, Social Critique, and Literary Form in the Sea Novels of Herman Melville* (Chapel Hill, NC: University of North Carolina Press, 1986).

A. McCann, *Cultural Politics in the 1790s: Literature, Radicalism and the Public Sphere* (New York: Palgrave, 1999).

T. McGowan, 'Two Forms of Fetishism: From the Commodity to Revolution in *Us*', *Galactica Media: Journal of Media Studies*, vol. 1, No. 1, (2019), 63–87.

T. McGowan, *University and Identity Politics* (New York: Columbia University Press, 2020).

H. Melville, 'Charles' Isle and the Dog-King', in Harrison Hayford (ed.), *Herman Melville* (New York: Library of America, 1984), pp. 788–792.

H. Melville, '*Benito Cereno*', in Dan McCall (ed.), *Melville's Short Novels* (New York: W.W. Norton, 2001), pp. 34–102.

S. Mihic, '"The End Was in the Beginning": Melville, Ellison, and the Democratic Death of Progress in *Typee* and *Omoo*,' in Jason Frank (ed.), *A Political Companion to Herman Melville* (Lexington, KY: University of Kentucky, 2014), n.p. Accessed as eBook.

J. Miller, *Can Democracy Work?* (New York: Picador, 2018).

T. Morrison, *Playing in the Dark: Whiteness and the Literary Imagination* (New York: Vintage Books, 1992).

C. Mouffe, 'Politics and Passions: The Stakes of Democracy', *Ethical Perspectives*, vol. 7, no. 2 (2000), 146–150.

C. Mouffe, *Agonistics: Thinking the World Politically* (London: Verso, 2013).

J. Olson, *The Abolition of White Democracy* (Minneapolis, MN: University of Minnesota Press, 2004).

J. Oppenheimer, *Private Demons: The Life of Shirley Jackson* (New York: Ballantine Books, 1989).

T. Paine, 'The Rights of Man, Part 1', in Eric Foner (ed.), *Thomas Paine: Collected Writings* (New York: Library of America, 1995), pp. 433–540.

R.R. Palmer, *The Age of the Democratic Revolution* (Princeton, NJ: Princeton University Press, 1969).

R. Paulson, *Representations of Revolution: 1789–1820* (New Haven, CT: Yale University Press, 1987).

M. Plot, *The Aesthetico-Political: The Question of Democracy in Merleau-Ponty, Arendt, and Ranciere* (New York: Bloomsbury, 2014).

E.A. Poe, 'The Imp of the Perverse', in George G. Harrap (ed.), *Poe's Tales of Mystery and Imagination* (New York: Weathervane Books, 1935), pp. 11–17.

E.A. Poe, 'The System of Doctor Tarr and Professor Fether', in Patrick Quinn (ed.), *Edgar Allan Poe: Poetry and Tales* (New York: Library of America, 1984), pp. 699–716.

E.A. Poe, 'Colloquy of Monos and Una', in Patrick Quinn (ed.), *Edgar Allan Poe: Poetry and Tales* (New York: Library of America, 1984a), pp. 449–457.

E.A. Poe, 'Mellonta Tauta', in Patrick Quinn (ed.), *Edgar Allan Poe: Poetry and Tales* (New York: Library of America, 1984b), pp. 871–885.

E.A. Poe, 'The Pit and the Pendulum', in Patrick Quinn (ed.), *Edgar Allan Poe: Poetry and Tales* (New York: Library of America, 1984c), pp. 491–506.

E.A. Poe, 'William Wilson', in Patrick Quinn (ed.), *Edgar Allan Poe: Poetry and Tales* (New York: Library of America, 1984d), pp. 337–357.

J. Rancière, *Dis-Agreement: Politics and Philosophy*, trans. Julie Rose (Minneapolis, MN: University of Minnesota Press, 1999).

J. Rancière, 'Democracies against Democracy: An Interview with Eric Hazon', in Amy Allen (ed.), *Democracy in What State?* trans. William McCuaig (New York: Columbia University Press, 2011), pp. 76–81.

S. Roberts, *Gothic Subjects: The Transformation of Individualism in American Fiction* (Philadelphia, PA: University of Pennsylvania Press, 2014).

R. Rodriguez, 'Sovereign Authority and the Democratic Subject in Poe', *Edgar Allan Poe Studies*, vol. 44 (2016), 39–56.

E. Roosevelt, *The Moral Basis of Democracy* (New York: Open Road, 2016).

R. Rorty, *Achieving Our Country* (Cambridge, MA: Harvard University Press, 1997).

J. Rousseau, 'The Social Contract', in John T. Scott (ed.), *The Major Political Writings of Jean-Jacques Rousseau* (Chicago, IL: University of Chicago Press, 2014), pp. 153–273.

A. Schlesinger, *A Pilgrim's Progress: Orestes A. Brownson* (Boston, MA: Little, Brown, 1966).

C. Sederholm, 'Raising Her Voice: Stephen King's Literary Dialogue with Shirley Jackson', in Kristopher Woofter (ed.), *Shirley Jackson: A Companion*, (New York: Peter Lang, 2021), pp. 59–73.

M. Smith, *The First Forty Years of Washington Society* (New York: Scribner's Sons, 1906).

S. Smith, 'What Kind of Democrat Was Spinoza?' *Political Theory*, vol. 33, no. 1 (2005), 6–27.

A. Stocker, 'Brown and the Godwinites', in P. Barnard, Hilary Emmett, and Stephen Shapiro (eds.), *The Oxford Handbook of Charles Brockden Brown* (Oxford: Oxford University Press, 2019), pp. 273–288.

C. Baxley, *Storm of the Century*, DVD (Los Angeles, CA: Warner Bros, 1999) Television.

J.L. Talmon, *The Origins of Totalitarian Democracy* (New York: W.W. Norton, 1970).

A. Taylor, *Democracy May Not Exist, but We'll Miss It When It's Gone* (New York: Metropolitan Books, 2019).

A. Tocqueville, *Ancien Regime and the Revolution*, trans. Gerald Bevan (New York: Penguin, 2008).

J. Tompkins, *Sensational Designs: The Cultural Work of American Fiction, 1790–1860*(Oxford: Oxford University Press, 1986).

M. Unger, '"Dens of Iniquity and Holes of Wickedness": George Lippard and the Queer City', *Journal of American Studies*, vol. 43, no. 2 (2009), 319–339.

J. Peele, *Us*, DVD (Hollywood, CA: Universal Pictures, 2009).

W. M. Verhoeven, '"This Blissful Period of Intellectual Liberty": Transatlantic Radicalism and Enlightened Conservatism in Brown's Early Writings', in Philip Barnard, Mark Kamrath, and Stephen Shapiro (eds.), *Revising Charles Brockden Brown: Culture, Politics, and Sexuality in the Early Republic* (Knoxville, TN: University of Tennessee Press, 2004), pp. 7–40.

C. West, *Democracy Matters: Winning the Fight against Imperialism* (New York: Penguin 2005).

W. Whitman, *Democratic Vistas: Original Edition in Facsimile*, Ed Folsom (ed.) (Iowa City, IA: University of Iowa, 2010).

S. Wilentz, *The Rise of American Democracy: Jefferson to Lincoln* (New York: W.W. Norton, 2005).

C. Wiltse, 'King Andrew', in James Bugg (ed.), *Jacksonian Democracy: Myth or Reality?* (New York: Holt, Rinehart and Winston, 1962), pp. 62–72.

M. Wollstonecraft, *The Vindications of the Rights of Woman: Norton Critical Edition* (New York: W.W. Norton, 1988).

G. Wood, *The Radicalism of the American Revolution* (New York: Vintage Books, 1991).

L. Ziff, *Literary Democracy: The Declaration of Cultural Independence in America* (New York: Viking Press, 1981).

S. Žižek, *The Sublime Object of Ideology,* 2nd ed. (London: Verso, 2009).

S. Žižek, 'Introduction', in Jean Ducange (ed.), *Robespierre: Virtue and Terror* (London: Verso, 2017), pp. vii–li.

Dedicated to
My English Teachers Along the Way

Cambridge Elements ⁼

The Gothic

Dale Townshend
Manchester Metropolitan University

Dale Townshend is Professor of Gothic Literature in the Manchester Centre for Gothic Studies, Manchester Metropolitan University.

Angela Wright
University of Sheffield

Angela Wright is Professor of Romantic Literature in the School of English at the University of Sheffield and co-director of its Centre for the History of the Gothic.

Advisory Board

About the Series

Seeking to publish short, research-led yet accessible studies of the foundational 'elements' within Gothic Studies as well as showcasing new and emergent lines of scholarly enquiry, this innovative series brings to a range of specialist and non-specialist readers some of the most exciting developments in recent Gothic scholarship.

Cambridge Elements ☰

The Gothic

Elements in the Series

Printed in the United States
by Baker & Taylor Publisher Services